**Indian River County Main Library**
**1600 21st Street**
**Vero Beach, FL 32960**

# TIMBERLINE BONANZA

Center Point
Large Print

Also by Allan Vaughan Elston and available from Center Point Large Print:

*Saddle Up for Steamboat*

**This Large Print Book carries the
Seal of Approval of N.A.V.H.**

# TIMBERLINE BONANZA

## Allan Vaughan Elston

CENTER POINT LARGE PRINT
THORNDIKE, MAINE

This Center Point Large Print edition is published
in the year 2016 by arrangement with
Golden West Literary Agency.

First US edition: Lippincott.
First UK edition: Ward Lock.

The text of this Large Print edition is unabridged.
In other aspects, this book may vary
from the original edition.
Printed in the United States of America
on permanent paper.
Set in 16-point Times New Roman type.

ISBN: 978-1-68324-115-7 (hardcover)
ISBN: 978-1-68324-119-5 (paperback)

Library of Congress Cataloging-in-Publication Data

Names: Elston, Allan Vaughan, 1887–1976, author.
Title: Timberline bonanza / Allan Vaughan Elston.
Description: Center Point Large Print edition. | Thorndike, Maine :
Center Point Large Print, 2016.
Identifiers: LCCN 2016024187| ISBN 9781683241157
    (hardcover : alk. paper) | ISBN 9781683241195 (pbk. : alk. paper)
Subjects: LCSH: Large type books. | GSAFD: Western stories.
Classification: LCC PS3509.L77 T56 2016 | DDC 813/.52—dc23
LC record available at https://lccn.loc.gov/2016024187

To my friend and counselor
through forty years,
WILL F. PLUMMER
of Missouri and points west

# TIMBERLINE
# BONANZA

# One

The sheriff and the city marshal idled in front of the Bank of Leadville, arguing a point of jurisdiction. "Look, Duggan," Sheriff Tucker said, "there's no county law against it. If it's a *town* ordinance that Croddy's violatin', go ahead and crack down on him."

"There's no ordinance agin stuffed bears," Duggan admitted, staring sourly across Chestnut Street at a fiercely lifelike grizzly posed upright in front of Chick Croddy's cigar store. "It's Croddy's neighbors that are complainin'," Duggan said. "And you can't blame 'em. Look at their hitchracks."

The hitchrails in front of Duffy's Bar and the Bon Ton pool hall were empty. Croddy's cigar shop, squeezed in between them, didn't have a hitchrail. Its customers were mainly local clerks and smelter hands who came unmounted. The saloon and pool hall relied a good deal on mounted trade from mines and lumber camps. And a rider wasn't likely to tie his horse face to face with what looked like a rampant grizzly bear. The wild animal smell was still strong on the beast's hide.

Sheriff Tucker curled a tongue in his cheek. "If

I was you, Duggan, I'd advise Croddy to get rid of it and put up a wooden Indian. If he don't, his neighbors'll sue hell out of him."

Tucker, big and florid and easygoing, was an opposite to the wiry and unsmiling Duggan. Between them they shared an immense responsibility; for Leadville, during these last twenty months, had mushroomed from nothing to forty thousand people. So far during this boom year of 1879 its mines had produced a ton of solid silver per day. The lure of it had flooded the town with gamblers, footpads, bunco men and hard women. Both jails, city and county, were full. According to the *Leadville Daily Chronicle*, during this month of August the district had averaged a killing per night.

Small wonder that Tucker declined to get excited about a mere stuffed bear.

"Listen!" Duggan exclaimed. "Was that a gunshot?"

The sound had come from a block or so up Harrison Avenue, which crossed Chestnut here at the Bank of Leadville. Looking that way they saw a man dash out of a gambling hall pursued by a second man who was brandishing a gun. Pursued and pursuer took off up Harrison toward the Clarendon Hotel.

"If it ain't one thing it's another," Duggan muttered, and hurried that way himself.

Ahead of him the pursuer fired a shot, missing,

but causing the sidewalk crowd to scatter. Duggan made no effort to catch up. He felt sure that one of his several constables would intercept and collar the gunman. Nor did he expect Tucker to follow. Except where there was a fatal shooting, the county officers usually let the city force handle the bar quarrels.

A block ahead of him Duggan saw Constable Monte Murray step out of a doorway and trip the gun-wielding pursuer. By the time Duggan got there the man had been disarmed and handcuffed.

"It was a row over some wine girl," Murray reported.

"Lock him up, Monte."

After the constable had hustled his prisoner away Duggan relaxed, watching the street traffic. Ore carts passed him, hauling pay rock to the smelters. A snowy skyline to the east marked the Mosquito Range, while the Continental Divide raised lofty summits directly west of the town. It was hard to believe that two years ago there'd been no town; and that this broad avenue of commerce had been only a pack trail winding up a gulch.

For now, directly behind Duggan, stood the handsome Daniels & Fisher Drygoods store, Leadville branch of the largest department store in Denver. Across from him was the new three-story Clarendon Hotel, with mining men, drummers and speculators crowding its lobby.

Next to the Clarendon the ornate Tabor Opera House was nearing completion.

Mayor Bill James, a carnation in his buttonhole, came along and spoke to Duggan. "Ever figure out that Bryson killing? I mean who did it and why?"

The city marshal shook his head. "It's got Tucker stumped too." A few nights ago Frank Bryson had been shot dead in an alley. Not a footpad job, for the man's pocket cash was still on him. Bryson, a newcomer here, had been a pleasant, sober man. Usually the Leadville killings had clear, raw motives involving money or women. A mystery murder like Bryson's was a rarity.

"That's a right smart span of mules," the mayor remarked as a mule-drawn spring wagon rattled by.

"A bit skittish," Duggan commented. "They ain't been broke to harness very long, I'd say."

The man driving the spring wagon had a hard, bony face which the marshal couldn't recall having seen before. A tarpaulin covered the wagon bed and a bulge there might be the dressed carcass of a deer which the man was protecting from sun and flies. Idly the marshal and the mayor watched the outfit rattle on down Harrison, its mules at a fast trot.

Three blocks below, at the Chestnut corner, Sheriff Tucker saw it coming. He was still in

12

front of the Bank of Leadville but had now been joined by young Barry Holden, leg man for the *Chronicle*.

"A spanking team," the reporter remarked.

As the spring wagon drew nearer the sheriff agreed. It reached the corner and turned west down Chestnut, the high-stepping mules scarcely breaking stride. Something about the driver seemed vaguely familiar to the sheriff. He was half sure he'd seen that hard bony face before. Where? On a Wanted poster?

Forty yards after making the turn the team came abreast of Chick Croddy's cigar store.

"Wow! They're off to the races!" yelled Barry Holden. "Look at 'em go!"

One glimpse and one smell of a stuffed grizzly bear was all the mules needed. The sudden spurt from a trot to a mad, headlong flight took the driver by surprise and almost toppled him from his seat. His right hand retained its grip on a rein but the other rein was jerked free from his left. "Whoa there!" he shouted helplessly.

One rein was worse than none at all. The spring wagon went careening on down Chestnut, a street which slanted sharply to the west. Panic kept the mules at a breakneck gallop.

Traffic made way for them. As the wagon wheeled recklessly past the Grand Hotel a sidewalk crowd there cheered lustily. It only made the mules run faster. Sheriff Tucker, back at the

Harrison Avenue corner, foresaw that a smashup was inevitable. With Barry Holden he hurried that way.

"They won't stop this side of Malta," Barry predicted. Malta was a smelter town three miles down the Arkansas River.

"The mules won't maybe," Tucker puffed, "but the wagon will. Look! It's turned over."

Saloon and hotel crowds, swarming into the street, nearly obscured the wreck. But Sheriff Tucker, panting as he sped toward it, had seen the mules veer to avoid head-on collision with a bull train plodding upgrade. The veer had failed by a few inches to clear a forewheel of the oncoming freight wagon and the shock of impact had fairly torn the lighter spring wagon from its moorings.

Over the heads of the crowd Tucker saw the panicked mules still running on, dragging trace chains and a broken singletree.

"Bet it busted the driver's neck!" Barry Holden said. He raced on with the sheriff at his heels.

They crossed Pine Street and a block beyond came to the wreck. A crowd circled it and Tucker, pushing through, heard a man ask, "Is he dead?"

"Looks like it," another man said, and Tucker supposed he meant the luckless driver.

The wagon lay on its side with a forewheel sheared off. And to the sheriff's astonishment, the wreck's casualty wasn't the driver. He failed to see the driver anywhere.

The wagon bed tarpaulin, and what it had covered, had been thrown clear of the wreck. On the ground lay a man Tucker had never seen before. He looked young, not over twenty-three, and there was a gag in his mouth. His wrists and ankles were bound securely with rawhide cords. He lay in the dust, eyes glazed, like a man struck dead.

But Tucker, kneeling by him, discovered that he wasn't dead. The young man was stunned and the sheriff, after a quick examination, concluded that he'd been unconscious even before the wreck.

A gash on his scalp wasn't fresh. Blood had caked over the wound, indicating that he'd been clubbed at least an hour ago. His pockets were empty. Tucker untied him, took the gag from his mouth.

"What happened to the driver?" he demanded.

Most of the onlookers didn't know. It had all happened so suddenly. Then a smelter hand who'd been among the first to reach the wreck spoke up. "When I got here a guy was pickin' himself out of the dust. Said somethin' about goin' fer a doctor. I seen him grab a horse from the nearest hitchrack and make off. He was out of sight before I noticed this other guy was all tied up."

The sheriff looked both ways along the street. "He lit out for parts unknown, I'll bet. Likely he was haulin' this boy to the river to dump him in;

or maybe to some deep mine shaft." His eyes searched the crowd and found two men he could trust. "Danniger, you and Clayburn ask up and down the street and try to find out which way he went. Everybody else take a good look at this boy and see if you can put a name to him."

The circle of bystanders looked at the wreck's victim and one by one shook their heads. Then, belatedly, Barry Holden himself recognized him.

"He came in on a stage this morning from End-of-Track," Barry remembered. "I met the stage thinking maybe Haw Tabor'd be on it. I saw this young fellow go into the Clarendon and register."

"Did he have any baggage?"

"Likely he did. But I didn't notice. He looked some different then. Had on a gunbelt and a cowboy hat."

The gunbelt and the hat were gone now. But the unconscious man still wore the scuffed half-boots of a range rider.

"Since he has a room at the Clarendon," Tucker decided, "we'll take him there. Barry, go fetch a cab and bring along Doctor Fowler. I'll meet you at this boy's room in an hour."

The sheriff spent the hour in a vain effort to trace the flight of the escaping driver. "But we found out where he got the mules and the spring wagon," Danniger reported. "They belong to Leitzman's livery barn at the foot of Pine." According to Leitzman, the man with the hard bony face had rented the rig for the day, paying cash.

At the Clarendon Hotel the desk clerk was expecting Tucker. "You can go right up, Sheriff. It's room 278."

"They got here all right?"

The clerk nodded. "About twenty minutes ago, Barry Holden and Doc Fowler. We took that cowboy Collier up to his room. They gave him a drink of whisky in the cab."

"Is that his name—Collier?"

"Take a look for yourself." The clerk whirled the registry book toward Tucker. "Top line, Sheriff." The top line registration of today's page was "John Collier, Denver."

Tucker was moving toward the stairs when a curious question from the clerk called him back. "Say, what's the connection between young Collier and Frank Bryson?"

Tucker asked alertly, "What makes you think there is one?"

"Because when this cowboy registered he asked what room Frank Bryson was in. I told him Bryson was picked up dead in an alley a few nights back. It was the first he'd heard of it. He gave me a blank stare, started to say something, swallowed it, then paid for a week in advance and went on up to his room. An hour later he went out, still with his gun on. Next time I saw him was when Doc Fowler and Barry Holden brought him in here, about twenty minutes ago."

Tucker hurried upstairs. Bryson, he knew, had been a guest at the Clarendon during his short stay in Leadville. It was clear that John Collier had expected to meet him here.

In room 278 the sheriff found the victim of the runaway wagon wreck lying on the bed with a doctor and a reporter on either side of him. The young man's eyes were open and he was fully conscious. The eyes were brown and matched close-cropped brown hair. His sun-tanned face had good looks and to Tucker it also seemed to have character.

"Can I question him, Doctor?"

"Go right ahead," Fowler consented. "But it won't do you any good."

Tucker asked bluntly: "Look, Collier; who batted you down and hauled you away in a wagon?"

"Why do you call me Collier?" The brown eyes had a vague stare but Tucker could see no guile in them. "Was I in a wagon? I can't remember."

"If your name's not Collier, what is it?"

"I don't know."

"Why did you come to Leadville? Was it to see Frank Bryson?"

"Is this Leadville? I can't remember anyone named Bryson."

"What *do* you remember?"

The young man who'd registered as John

Collier closed his eyes and furrowed his forehead. He appeared to be in sincere concentration. "I remember riding in a hack. Someone gave me a drink of whisky. Then they brought me to this room."

The sheriff turned to Fowler. "Is he faking, Doctor?"

"Not at all," Fowler answered. "A case of complete amnesia, I'd say."

"How long will he be this way?"

"Who knows? A day, a week, a month—a year maybe. He had two bad shocks. The first when someone hit him on the head; the second an hour or so later when he was piled up in a wreck."

Tucker curled a tongue in his plump, rubicund cheek and looked down at the man on the bed. "The wreck saved your life, I figure. Whoever was haulin' you away meant to get rid of you for keeps. Take it easy, boy. I'm hopin' you can remember things, by this time tomorrow."

# Two

But when tomorrow came he still couldn't remember. The doctor called first, re-examined the head wound and put on a fresh bandage. "They hit you with something round and blunt," Fowler concluded, "like a wagon spoke or a gun. Better

19

stay in your room for a day or two. I'll have your meals sent up."

Next came Sheriff Tucker and one of his deputies, an ex–trail hand named Cal Barstow. Barstow's tall range hat and saddle-bowed legs and slanting gunbelt made him distinctive in this cloud-high mining town.

He gave a freckled grin when Tucker presented him. "I figure you and me sort of belong on the same roundup, Collier."

"Only we don't think your name's Collier," Tucker said.

The brown eyes narrowed as they shifted from Tucker to Barstow. "You don't? Why?"

The sheriff lighted a stogie, then sat down with it uptilted in his mouth. "I checked through your baggage while you slept, yesterday. No identification except this." He held up a dress belt of narrow leather. The belt's buckle had a dim initial on it; the letter "W." "Chances are your name begins with a W. But till we learn better we might as well call you Collier."

"It ain't natural," Cal Barstow put in, "for a man's duffel not to have somethin' with his name on it. Like a receipted bill or a meal ticket or an old letter. We figger you ditched 'em yourself, overlookin' the belt, then picked the name Collier to hide your real one."

The man on the bed flushed. "So you think I'm a crook?"

"Nope," Tucker said. "It's more likely you came here to check on some devilment and wanted to keep under cover till you got the right answers."

"It's been done before," Cal Barstow said. "I used a phony name myself, one season, when I worked as a range detective out of Cheyenne."

"From a stage driver," Tucker went on, "we know you rode a train on the South Park Line from Denver to End-of-Track at Webster. There you changed to a Barlow and Sanderson stage-coach and were on it a full day and night, via Fair Play and Trout Creek Pass to Leadville. Two or three times on the trip the other passengers saw you take a letter from your pocket and read it through. The man next to you says the letter was on Clarendon Hotel stationery. Was it from Frank Bryson?"

To Collier the name meant nothing. "Sorry. I just can't remember anything that happened before you picked me out of that wreck."

Tucker puffed for a moment on his stogie. "The stage passengers saw you open your valise at the last relay stop before getting to Leadville. They say you exchanged your Sunday belt for a gun-belt. Shows you expected trouble at Leadville."

"And you sure as hell found it, pardner." Cal Barstow grinned as he licked the flap of a cigaret.

"When you paid in advance for your room here," the sheriff said, "the clerk had a fair look at your wallet. He saw money in it, a sheaf fat enough to be a couple hundred dollars. Whoever batted you down took that wallet, along with your gun and hat and pocket stuff."

"Plus the letter you were seen readin' on the stage," Cal added. "Must've been dynamite in that letter."

"Enough," Tucker agreed, "to make someone try to kill you."

Collier stared vacantly. "But how could they know I had it?"

The sheriff shrugged. "*Quien sabe*? Maybe you asked some question that made 'em leery. So they grabbed you, frisked you and found a letter from Bryson. They'd already taken care of Bryson; so now they had to get rid of you."

"How long had Bryson been here?"

"Only four or five days. But lots of mining men here had known him at other camps. They say he was honest as daylight. In his younger days he panned gravel in California; later he moved from camp to camp, sometimes working a claim, more often in recent years merely buying an interest in some promising mine and then selling it at a profit. He came directly here from Deadwood in the Black Hills."

"Did he invest in a Leadville property?"

"No. He just hired a saddle horse and rode around the district, keeping his eyes open. On the fourth evening when he left his horse at the livery barn he looked kinda excited.

'Whatsamatter, Mr. Bryson?' the barnman asked him. 'I just ran into somethin' big,' Bryson told him. 'So big it scares me.' He walked to the Clarendon, sat down in the lobby and wrote a letter, then walked to the post office to mail it. After supper he wrote a second letter and went out, probably to mail it at the post office. But he never got there. Next morning he was found dead in an alley."

More and more it confused John Collier. "You think the first letter was to me?"

"It fits. Think it over, boy. Maybe it'll open a window in your mind." The sheriff and his deputy went out, promising to return in the morning.

After sundown a hotel boy brought supper on a tray. "I fetched you the *Chronicle*, Mr. Collier."

As he ate, Collier read a review of all the known facts in both the Bryson mystery and his own. One new development was reported. "The man who drove the spring wagon, and who escaped on a stolen horse, has been identified from an old Wanted poster on file in Tucker's office. He is Gil Hocker, who broke jail at Tucson, Arizona, last March."

The issue quoted Doctor Fowler on John Collier's condition. "Loss of memory from shock, the doctor says, is usually temporary. There is a reasonable probability that the victim will be able to identify himself within a week or so. However, many amnesia cases have lasted much longer."

23

Collier picked up a narrow belt and stared helplessly at a "W" on the buckle. So his name could be West or Wilson or Watson! He tried to force his mind to a groping search for it. Where had he come from? Why was he here? What was his connection with Frank Bryson?

He pushed away the supper tray and continued reading. The news was mainly about local mines, with fabulous production figures tossed about lavishly. New millionaires were sprouting like weeds around Leadville. Collier read name after name on the chance it might jar his memory.

The most frequently mentioned name was H. A. W. Tabor. It seemed that Mr. Tabor owned both the *Little Pittsburgh* and the *Matchless,* the two richest mines in the district. He'd been successively postmaster, mayor, county commissioner, president of the Leadville Mining Exchange, and was now lieutenant governor of Colorado. Other silver kings mentioned were August Meyer, Flint Hammond, Fryer, Witherell and Vic Werner.

A boastful editorial caught Collier's eye and he read through it. "The richest little hill ever discovered in America is Fryer Hill, only a mile east of town. No area of like dimension in all history has ever equaled its production of precious metals. The Big Six of Fryer Hill are the *Little Pittsburgh,* the *Matchless,* the *Chrysolite,* the *Little Chief,* the *Climax* and the *Robert E Lee.*

Latest smelter figures indicate that Flint Hammond's *Morning Star,* in Big Strayhorse Gulch, may soon join that select group."

The endless superlatives cloyed on Collier. He learned that less than a year after the first cabin was built on Harrison Avenue, four thousand men were calling for mail each day at the General Delivery window of the post office. Now the city had seventeen smelters, four banks and eighty saloons. The three stage lines running into Leadville were using seven hundred horses, and were taking in $70,000.00 a month in passenger and express fares. All coaches were Concords with a capacity of from twelve to sixteen passengers.

"They say I came in on one myself," Collier murmured. "But I can't remember."

When it was dark he went to bed, hoping that a night's sleep would restore his memory.

After restless hours he awakened and three chimes from a bell tower told him it was three in the morning. But he could hear a clatter of street sounds. Revelers were still abroad.

The man with a bandaged head closed his eyes to seek sleep again. Then he heard a scratching at his room door. In a moment he knew that a key had been thrust stealthily into the lock. Fortunately the door was both locked and bolted.

As he became wider awake, John Collier realized that the sound didn't come from the hall door but from an interior door giving to an adjacent room. It permitted the two rooms to be rented *en suite*, if desired by a family or party of friends. The connecting door was locked, but Collier wasn't sure whether it was also bolted on this side.

His window blind was up and a dim moonlight came into the room. Getting quietly out of bed he crossed in his bare feet to the interior door. By peering closely he could see that it was secured by an iron slide bolt located about a foot above the knob. All the while a series of scratching sounds at the keyhole meant that key after key was being patiently tried.

Why? A moment's thought made it grimly clear to Collier. Whoever had hired Gil Hocker to haul him away in a spring wagon had more reason than ever to get rid of him now. A lost memory might be regained in a day or so; and when that happened, Collier could remember and accuse his assailants.

So they had to work fast. They'd sent another killer to finish the job. Someone who'd rented the next room, waiting there till three o'clock when the victim would surely be asleep!

There was a click as the lock turned. The man in the next room, with his ring of keys, had found one that fit.

But when he turned the knob and pushed, the door didn't give. Collier smiled in the gloom.

Would the man give up? He must have registered at the desk, so the clerk should know him by sight. Collier's natural impulse was to go down to the lobby and report the attempted intrusion.

But while he was gone the man might leave the room and escape by back stairs. He was almost certain to do that if he heard Collier go out into the hall. What about tangling with him alone?

John Collier didn't feel quite up to it. It was too soon after his bruisings of yesterday. In a rough-and-tumble he'd be likely to come off second best. He had nothing but his bare hands to fight with.

Then he heard another sound, stealthy and not at the keyhole. It came from about a foot above the doorknob—a soft churning sound in the thin veneer of the door's panel. The man had a brace-and-bit and was boring a hole, bolt-high. He'd come prepared with tools in case he found the door bolted.

The point of a half-inch bit came softly through the panel. Immediately it was withdrawn and a second hole bored tangent with the first. Collier put his finger to the wood and felt auger filings. It would take only a minute to bore each hole; and several adjacent holes would make room for a keyhole saw.

In short shift the man could remove a four-inch square of wood from the panel and through it could reach his hand and wrist. The hole was being cut slightly to the right of the iron slide bolt.

Reaching through, the man could slip the bolt and then enter the room at will.

All of it assumed that his intended victim was asleep. To keep him from knowing better John Collier was careful to make no sound as he began groping for a cord or a rope. A stout piece of flexible wire would do; anything about three feet long that could be twisted into a knot.

Finding it in the dim light wasn't easy. A struck match might be heard in the next room.

The man in there was now working on the fourth and last side of his four-inch square. If a hand were thrust through a hole, it could be caught and held fast like a wolf's paw in a trap.

Groping for a tie-rope, what Collier finally found was a narrow leather dress belt with the initial "W" on its buckle. He decided it would do nicely. By threading the end through the buckle he drew a loop just big enough to slip around a wrist.

With it he waited quietly by the door.

The boring was finished and the tip of a keyhole saw showed on one side of the square. The saw moved gently, trickling sawdust to the floor. A sleeper wouldn't have heard it.

One by one the saw cleared the four sides of the square. Then the square of thin wood was pulled carefully into the other room. The entire operation had been neat, swift and almost soundless.

A clenched hand, then a sleeveless wrist and

half a hairy forearm, came through the hole to grope for the slide bolt. It was easy for Collier to slip his noosed belt over it. He jerked it tight on the wrist and heard a howl of surprise and pain from beyond the door.

When the noose was as tight as he could pull it, Collier wrapped the other end of the belt around the door's knob and made a secure tie there.

He stepped back, struck a match and lighted an oil lamp. Thumps came from the door where the man struggled frantically to free himself. "The harder you pull," Collier told him, "the tighter you'll draw that noose."

There were kicks and choked oaths and then the man stopped struggling. His voice came with a crafty hoarseness. "What'll you take to let me go?"

The intruder himself, Collier reasoned, wasn't important. He'd be only a hireling, like Hocker who'd driven the mule-drawn spring wagon. "Okay. Tell me who put you up to this, and why, and I'll let you go."

There was a minute of sly silence. The man was scheming and Collier knew he couldn't trust his answer. The man would trump up any false name, and any false reason, to buy his release.

"It was Sol Lenniger," the trapped man confided. "He didn't tell me why."

"What were you supposed to do? Cut my throat or just beat my brains out?"

"Nothin' like that!" the man bleated. "Honest to Gawd! I was just gonna throw a scare into you so you'd leave town."

"That's a better deal than you gave Bryson."

Another scared silence. Then— "I didn't have nothin' to do with Bryson. Let me go. You promised. . . ."

"This payoff man, Sol Lenniger. Did he use to live in Peoria, Illinois?"

"That's the one. Now let me go, quick, before someone comes."

"Peoria, Illinois," Collier told him, "is just a name I'm reading off a wall calendar. It advertises a harness factory there."

A volley of cursings came through the door.

Down the hallway other doors opened. From the corridor came voices. "What's going on in 278? Hi, in there; anything wrong?"

"Yes." 278's inmate raised his own voice. "I trapped a wolf. Mind reporting it to the night clerk? Ask him to send for the sheriff."

# Three

By nine in the morning all of Leadville was buzzing about this second attempt on the life of John Collier. Angela Rand, riding a horse-drawn omnibus down Harrison Avenue on her way to work, heard the story being tossed back and forth by other passengers.

"They say he still don't know who he is."

"Or where he came from, Ed. But somebody's sure out to get that boy. A guy sawed a hole through his door last night and tried to knife him."

"You got it wrong, Elmer. The guy didn't have a knife on him. But he had a garroter's strap in his kit. He figured to choke the boy in his sleep."

Angela gave a slight shudder, yet continued to listen in fascination.

Elmer said: "They claim it's all tied up with that alley job the other night. I mean the gun job on a fella named Bryson. It was a letter from Bryson, they say, that brought young Collier to Leadville."

"Which ain't his name, Elmer. His real name begins with W."

"Does he look anything like Bryson? I mean enough like him to be kin?"

"Nope. This Collier boy's about five foot ten with brown eyes and light brown hair. A Nordic type, they say; might come from English or Canadian stock; or maybe Scotch. Bryson was short and wide and shaggy; agate-black eyes and bushy brows."

The description of Bryson made Angela Rand thoughtful. It stirred a memory and might mean something. She decided to take the morning off. No reason she shouldn't, since she wasn't a paid worker. Her father, Milton Rand, was county clerk and his office, these boom days, was sadly understaffed. Sometimes Angela volunteered to help out there as a filer or copy clerk.

Traffic was thick as the omnibus, with stops at each corner, threaded its way through every manner of horse-drawn vehicle—ore carts, freight wagons, buggies, buckboards, hacks, surreys, here and there an open clarence with matched trotters. Some of the new silver kings liked to show off and fancy rigs made a good way to do it. A sixteen-passenger Concord stood in front of the Clarendon ready to pull out for End-of-Track. Across from it an ox wagon was unloading stone blocks for the new Tabor Opera House.

Lake County as yet owned no courthouse building. Pending construction of one the county offices were housed in a number of rented frame buildings on lower Harrison. The one used by the county clerk was at the Elm Street corner and Angela, getting out there, went instead to Sheriff Tucker's office across the street.

The sheriff wasn't in. "Him and Cal Barstow are up at the Clarendon, Miss Rand. They're gettin' the dope about last night from that fella Collier."

Curiosity to see Collier lured Angela. A cloak of mystery veiled him and it might be that she herself could throw light on it. She went out to the street where the omnibus had turned around and was ready to return up Harrison.

Angela reboarded it and rode four blocks to

the Clarendon. Its lobby, as she entered it, was milling and humming as usual. Speculators, mine promoters, fortune hunters, gamblers, merchants, politicians and engineers; some had sent east for their families and Angela saw a sprinkling of women in flounced skirts and feathered hats.

A sleek, ruddy man tipped his fedora. "Good morning, Angela. Anything I can do for you?"

"Nothing, Mr. Janford." He was a title lawyer who hung around the county offices a good deal. Twice he'd tried to date Angela and she was sure she didn't like him.

In fact Angela disliked the entire courthouse atmosphere. She was trying to persuade her father to give up his billet as county clerk and take a job in a bank. He wouldn't earn nearly as much, of course, because here in Lake County the fee system was in vogue. County officers received no salaries but were paid in fees directly from the public. During the last twelve months fees paid to the county clerk totaled sixty thousand dollars; and to the sheriff fifty thousand. Out of that Angela's father had to pay his clerks and the sheriff had to pay his deputies. Fees ran high at an office where men stood in line daily to put new mining claims on record, to record transfers of old ones and deeds to city lots.

And Angela Rand, who until three months ago had been a student at the University of Missouri, had been taught by her political science professor that the fee system bred corruption. She knew her father was incorruptible. Just the same she wished he was out of there.

To avoid Janford she went over to a young man she liked much better. He was Barry Holden of the *Chronicle.* "Hi, pretty one," he greeted breezily. "First time I've seen you since Flint Hammond's party. Looks like he's getting ready to throw another one." The reporter looked toward a group across the lobby.

Angela saw Flint Hammond in a circle of Leadville's elite. Both men and women were in the group and Hammond's handsome, shock-haired head showed above all others. He was Leadville's newest millionaire and richest bachelor, who only a year ago had had nothing but muscle and a will to win. Now his *Morning Star* mine had flooded him with fortune. He kept a suite here at the Clarendon; and last week he'd entertained a hundred guests in the Clarendon's ballroom, importing an orchestra from Denver.

"It was a slam-bang blowout," Barry remembered, "even if you did turn me down to go with Vic Werner." He added slyly, "But Vic's in Fair Play today, so what about you meeting me here for lunch?"

"I'll be glad to," Angela agreed. Her eyes were on the stairs watching for Sheriff Tucker. If he didn't come down in a few minutes she'd go up to him.

Waiting, she asked suddenly, "What do you think of the fee system, Barry, under which the county pays its officers?"

The question caught the reporter by surprise but he answered frankly. "It's only half bad, Angela; but the fine-and-license system, that the city uses, is rotten all the way through."

That she could hardly doubt. Here in Leadville the city government was mainly supported by selling licenses to saloons and gambling halls, and by collecting the automatic weekly fines which were assessed to all prostitutes.

"There it goes again!" Barry exclaimed dismally. "No rest for a news hawk." He'd heard a gunshot from the street and went out to cover it.

Angela went to the lobby desk where the night clerk, now off duty, was still standing by to retell his adventure of the night. A knot of idlers were hanging on his words. "It was a sight for sore eyes! There was this cowboy Collier, at three in the morning, sitting on the bed smoking a cigaret; and grinning at a hand stuck through a hole in a door. Somebody in the next room was kicking the door and cussing like crazy. So I unlocked 276 and went in by its hall door. And there was the other guy as helpless as a shoat in a chute. He had a kitful of tools; one of them was a strangler's strap he hadn't got to use yet. Maddest guy I ever saw!"

"How did he get in there?" a man asked.

"Not by registering at the desk. An honest mine foreman happens to rent that room by the week. At midnight he got a phony message saying his shaft was flooded and the pumps wouldn't work. So he rode out to the *Little Eva,* where he runs things, and found he'd been buncoed. The note was just to get him out of the room."

Angela spoke to the clerk on duty. "Is Sheriff Tucker upstairs? I'd like to see him."

The day clerk was young and more than willing to serve a pretty girl like Angela Rand. "Sure. Room 278. I'll take you up there myself. Watch the desk, Tom, till I get back."

He came out and offered his arm to Angela. She went with him up the wide, carpeted stairs. "Mr. Bush is fit to be tied," he chuckled.

"Because of last night?" Angela knew that Mr. William Bush was the proud proprietor of the Clarendon, a host acutely sensitive about any intrusion on the comfort and privacy of his guests.

"Yeh, it like to started a panic this morning; folks hearing about a prowling strangler who saws through doors at three a.m."

"What's the man's name?"

"Calls himself Murdy. A sharper who used to deal blackjack on lower Chestnut. He's in jail right now waiting a hearing before Judge Updegraff."

In room 278 they found a carpenter putting in a new interior door under the supervision of Proprietor Bush.

"Collier's using 277, across the hall, till we get through here," Bush said.

In room 277 they found a slim young man with brown-eyed good looks and a bandaged head. With him was a county deputy whom Angela knew and liked quite well. "Hello, Cal. Where's Sheriff Tucker?"

Cal Barstow stood up on his bowed legs and grinned at her. "He went out fer nourishment and a couple headache pills. He's been up since half past three and he's about played out. Angela, meet my roommate, Johnnie Collier. Johnnie, this here's the most popular gal in Lake County and you'll need to stand in line to get a date with her."

"I better get back to my desk," the day clerk said, and reluctantly left them.

Angela smiled and held out her hand. The young stranger who took it didn't miss the blueness of her eyes or the brightness of her coiled yellow hair. "I already know a good deal about you, Mr. Collier."

"I wish *I* did," Collier said.

She decided by his voice that he was western rather than southern. "Your roommate?" she asked curiously of Cal Barstow.

The deputy placed a chair for her and when she was seated he explained. "They've tried to get Johnnie twice, so they're a cinch to try again. The sheriff told me to move in with him till we nab whoever's back of it."

"You already have, haven't you? Murdy—and he's in jail."

"It was Murdy last night and Hocker yesterday. Next time it'll be someone else. Whoever's out to get Johnnie ain't playin' fer peanuts."

"You think it's the same people who killed Mr. Bryson?"

"We'd bet on it."

John Collier fixed a puzzled gaze on the girl, wondering why she'd come. "Do you know anything about Bryson?" he asked her.

"I read what was in the papers," Angela told them. "But I never heard anyone describe him till this morning. They say he was short, wide and shaggy, with black eyes and bushy brows."

"That's him," Cal confirmed.

"I was helping out at the county clerk's office Friday morning," Angela said. "A man of that description came in and asked to see Book A of the 1878 mineral claim filings. I got it and he began looking through it. Anyone can look at a record ledger, provided he doesn't take it out of the office."

"Which filing," Cal asked keenly, "did he want to see?"

"I have no idea. More than a thousand claim filing are recorded in that book and he could have been interested in any of them. In a little while he gave the book back to me and asked to see Book B of the 1879 transfers. I got it for him and he spent half an hour looking through it, there at the counter. It's something that happens every day. I'd have thought nothing of it except that this man called me and asked if he could borrow a reading glass."

"A readin' glass!" Cal Barstow exclaimed. "You mean a magnifyin' glass like they use to read fine, dim print?"

"That's it. I loaned him the one we keep at the office. A few minutes later he returned it with the ledger, and went out."

"Did he say anything?"

"Not a word. I forgot all about him till I heard someone describe him this morning."

The door opened and Proprietor Bush looked in. "Number 278's ready for you, Mr. Collier."

"Thanks." They crossed the hall to the room originally assigned to John Collier. A new interior door had been hung.

The hotel man gave a wry apology. "Please don't judge us by the outrage last night, Mr. Collier. I guarantee it won't happen again."

Cal Barstow tapped the butt of his gun and said cockily, "If it does, I'll be ready for it."

"Anything we can do for you, just speak up," Bush offered.

"In that case," Cal said, "you might ask the kitchen to send us up a pot of coffee."

"It'll be right up," Bush promised.

Cal closed the door after him. He placed the

room's rocker for Angela and then sat on the bed with Collier.

Immediately the three resumed discussion of Frank Bryson.

"So he found something!" Angela concluded. "I mean in one of those ledgers."

"A phony entry?" Cal guessed.

"Maybe a forged filing," John Collier suggested.

"But a forgery," Angela objected, "wouldn't show in the ledger. When a person wants to record a filing or a title, he brings the paper in and leaves it with the county clerk. The county clerk has it copied word for word in a record book, then attests it as a true copy with his own signature. Ultimately he returns the paper to the person who brought it in, who takes it home to keep in a safe place. If a member of the public wants to examine a title, he's always free to look at the true copy on record."

So forgery or an illegal substitution of names wouldn't show on the record. Usually an original title paper would have two signatures, those of a seller and a notary public. These signatures would be copied into the ledger by a clerk. The only direct signature showing in the ledger would be that of Angela's father, attesting that the entry was a true copy.

"So why," John Collier puzzled, "would Bryson need a magnifying glass?"

On that score Angela was equally confused.

Bryson would know that the handwriting in the ledger was merely that of a copy clerk; to find an erasure or a substitution he'd need to look at the original title paper.

"We'd better have a peep at that page, anyway," Cal muttered.

"What page?" Angela questioned. "Book B of 1879 has hundreds of transfers: store buildings, town lots, mining claims, leases bought and sold. Mr. Bryson had a certain property in mind, but we don't."

"He was there Friday morning," Cal said. "Friday afternoon he rented a horse and rode into the hills. Got back at nightfall, wrote a letter, mailed it at the post office. After supper he paced the lobby for a spell, then wrote a second letter. On the way to mail it he was dragged into an alley and shot."

"Why would he walk to the post office?" Collier asked. "Isn't there a box for outgoing mail right on the lobby desk?"

Cal chewed on it for a while. "Maybe someone had an eye on him, Johnnie, and he knew it. So he didn't trust an open box on the lobby desk. Reckon he figgered the only sure way to get that letter in the mails was to take it to the post office himself."

"If we knew where he went on that last afternoon ride," Angela said, "we might be halfway to the answer."

"Tucker's got Gerry Harlan workin' on that," Cal said. To Collier he explained, "Gerry's our ace deputy."

Angela looked dismally at John Collier's bandaged head. "They tried twice to kill you. And no wonder! They know that any minute you may get your memory back and when you do . . ."

"When you do they're sunk," Cal cut in grimly. "That's why they're out after you, pardner. Dead men don't remember."

There was a knock at the door and a white-coated waiter came in with a tray. The tray held the Clarendon's best silver service, a steaming coffeepot with matching cream pitcher and sugar bowl. Also there were three cups and a plate of cakes. "Compliments of Mr. Bush." The man set the tray on a table and went out.

"I'll serve," Angela Rand offered. She tried to look gay as she poured three cups. "Sugar, Mr. Collier?"

The man with a bandaged head said, "And cream, please."

"If you can't remember anything," Angela questioned, "how do you know you like it with cream?"

"Make mine black," Cal Barstow said.

The girl passed each man his cup and put sugar in her own. "How about a cookie, Cal?"

Barstow didn't take a cookie but Collier did. Then Cal Barstow raised his cup and said lightly:

"We mustn't let it spoil our appetites, Johnnie; because we're takin' Angela to lunch."

She divided a smile between them. "Sorry, boys. I've already promised Barry Holden."

Sheriff Tucker, having refreshed himself at the bar, came up the stairs. He turned a corner and moved with a heavy man's lumbering gait down the north wing corridor, knocking at room 278. When there was no answer he wondered if John Collier had disobeyed the doctor's orders by going out.

The door wasn't locked and the portly, full-faced sheriff pushed it open. What he saw petrified him. Two young men and a girl were in the room and nothing was right about them. The girl in the rocking chair had a drugged look. John Collier got to his feet with his face blank and his eyes stupid. He reached for a bedpost to steady himself, then collapsed to the floor beside Cal Barstow.

Angela Rand and John Collier, who'd each nibbled a cake with only a single sip from the cup, were merely sick and cloudy-headed. But Cal Barstow, who'd taken several lusty swallows, was past help. The sheriff of Lake County, kneeling by his favorite deputy, found him already dead.

# Four

When he was able to think at all John Collier's overwhelming mood was fury. The first two murder tries had endangered only himself. But this one had cost the life of Cal Barstow. It might just as easily have destroyed Angela Rand.

"I'm going after those devils," he swore savagely to Tucker. "Give me Cal's badge and gun and let me go hunting for 'em. No use of me staying cooped up here like a sitting duck. I'd rather tangle with 'em in the open."

It was afternoon and the doctor had just left. Antidotes had nullified the effects of a poison. Angela had been taken to her home on Capitol Hill.

A leathery giant named Gerry Harlan was now with them. He was Tucker's senior deputy and had spent the last two days trying to trace the excursions of Bryson into the mine-pocked hills east of Leadville. Now he was assigned to supplant Cal Barstow as John Collier's roommate and bodyguard until the source of the threat could be identified.

The sheriff looked at Collier with a quizzical sympathy. "If I gave you a gun, how do you know you could use it?"

Collier couldn't answer that one any more than he'd been able to answer Angela's question about how he knew he liked cream in his coffee. "Try me and see," he said impatiently.

"You'll have to stay quiet at least one more night," Tucker said. "I promised Fowler you would. If you have a good night, tomorrow afternoon you can go on a prowl with me and Gerry."

"A prowl where?"

"On a still hunt for the fake waiter. He could be hanging out at any one of forty underworld joints on State or Chestnut. Those dives are crawling with gun-pullers like Hocker and Murdy and the fake waiter. You had a good look at the waiter, didn't you?"

"I'd know him anywhere. All I want is a shot at him."

"The real waiter," Gerry Harlan said, "can't help us any. He was coming along the hallway with a tray when someone yanked him into an empty room and knocked him cold. The guy took his white jacket and tray, doped the coffeepot and came on to 278."

"After delivering it," the sheriff went on, "he ditched the jacket and left by the back stairs. If he thinks you didn't get a good look at him he might show himself in some South Side dive. Tomorrow evening we'll make the rounds down there."

Collier fretted impatiently all through the night. In the morning the doctor called and was pleased with his patient's improvement. He took away the head bandage and left only a padded patch on the scalp. "It won't show under a hat," he said.

Then came the live-wire reporter, Barry Holden. He brought word that Angela Rand was fully recovered.

"Physically, I mean. Mentally she's still in a shock about Cal Barstow. Like everybody else she thought a lot of Cal. By the way, Collier, she sent you a note."

The note said:

Dear Mr. W.,
    It doesn't seem right to call you John Collier when I know that's not your name. Please be careful and do what the sheriff and the doctor say. If I can be of any help, please let me know.
Your friend,<br>
*Angela R*

It was mid-afternoon before Sheriff Tucker came in. "Try this on for size, boy." The gunbelt he tossed to Collier had a forty-five in its holster. "You won't need to use it, though. There'll be at least six of us."

He watched critically as Collier buckled on the belt, tying the holster string low on his right thigh. "You've done that before," he surmised. A high-crowned cowboy's hat hung from a wall peg and Tucker thumbed toward it. "Grab your hat and let's go."

"It's not mine," Collier said. He'd been picked up hatless from the wagon wreck and hadn't been outdoors since. The hat on the wall peg had been Cal Barstow's and whoever had taken Cal's things away had overlooked it.

"Put it on anyway," Tucker said. He handed the hat to Collier. "I've an idea it'll fit you in more ways than one."

Collier hesitated a moment, then put the hat on his head. "Just to let folks know that I'm on Cal's side; and for keeps."

With Gerry Harlan they went down to the lobby and found City Marshal Duggan waiting with two of his deputies, Murray and Moran. Duggan grimaced dubiously when he saw Collier. "You're jumpin' the gun a little, I'd say, after that runaway mule ride."

"We need him along," Tucker argued. "Of the six of us he's the only one who can point out that fake waiter."

The Clarendon lobby had the usual crowd and most of it fixed curious eyes on John Collier. Being three times a murder target within thirty-six hours made a record even for Leadville.

Barry Holden appeared and joined them. The reporter nodded toward the barroom. "Talk about your cold-blooded gamblers! Go in and see for yourself. One-card Connerly's posting a bet in there."

"How much and who with?" Harlan asked.

47

"It's for five thousand and he's making it with Vic Werner of the *Chrysolite.* They're putting up stakes with the barkeep right now."

"What," Collier asked, "are they betting on?"

"On your life, brother!" Barry lowered his voice. "It's that whoever's after you'll get you before you're a month older."

Neither Tucker nor Duggan seemed surprised. "Connerly'll bet on anything," the sheriff said. "Once I saw him spread molasses on a checkerboard and bet that the next fly would light on a black square."

They moved to the barroom archway but didn't go in. Two men at the bar were counting out money in big bills and taking receipts for it from the bartender. The terms of the wager were put in writing and sealed with the money in an envelope. "Connerly's the dressy guy with the diamond shirt stud," Barry told Collier. "Other's Vic Werner; he owns one of the Big Six on Fryer Hill."

"Always gives me the jeebies," Harlan said, "to see 'em throw money around like that."

John Collier's gaze shifted to two other men who were drinking at a side table. The obsequious attentions of a waiter indicated that they were men of importance. In a moment Barry identified them. "You're looking at number one and number two here in Leadville. The big good-looking fellow is Flint Hammond of the *Morning Star* mine; he could lose a ten-thousand dollar bet every Saturday night and not go broke. The other guy's got him topped a mile; he's Haw Tabor, the first lord of Fryer Hill. But Haw's more interested in politics right now. Already he's lieutenant governor and scheming to nudge his way into the U.S. Senate."

"Come on," Tucker said impatiently. "We won't find our man in a high-class bar like this."

They went out and turned south down Harrison. "We're hours too early," Duggan growled as they hit State Street. "These dives are tame, right now, compared to what they'll be at midnight."

Yet even at four in the afternoon the bars were full. "Look 'em over, Collier," Tucker said as they entered a saloon. "If you see that waiter, sing out."

After a quick inspection Collier shook his head. It was the same at the Come Again Bar, next door. A door beyond they went into the Odeon Dance Hall where Charlie Childs, the proprietor, came up with a whining protest. "What's the idea? I paid my license fee, didn't I?"

"It's no raid, Charlie," Duggan said. "We're just rat-hunting."

The rat who'd posed as a waiter wasn't in sight. Dancers were shuffling around the floor. Inspection from six armed officers drew only bold stares. "Look, we got company," a girl giggled to her partner. "They ain't after *you,* are they, honey-boy?"

The music stopped and a herder yelled, "Promenade to the bar, everybody."

The sheriff's party moved on through an arch-way where chips rattled in a dozen brace games. Again Collier failed to spot the fake waiter. "They had a riot in here last night," Duggan said. "Brass knucks and knives. One of my boys got a fractured skull trying to break it up."

By sundown they finished West State Street and then had supper at Gino's Restaurant on Pine. Light was fading when they got to the city jail at the foot of Pine. There the jailer came out with information. "We're about to lose Murdy," he reported.

"How?"

"Judge Updegraff set his bail at three thousand dollars. We didn't think he could raise that much cash. But he wrote a check for three thousand and passed it through the bars. We won't know till the bank opens whether it's good or not."

Tucker, after conferring with Duggan, made a decision. "If the check's good we'll accept it as bail. Then we'll tail Murdy and see where he goes. He might lead us to the payoff man."

To Collier it made sense. Murdy and Hocker and the waiter weren't really important. "We're after the guy who hired 'em," Gerry Harlan said.

The bars and gaming halls along West Chestnut kept them busy till nine o'clock. The stuffed bear was gone from in front of Croddy's cigar shop. "I made him get rid of it," Duggan said.

At the Comique Theater a sign advertised "Forty

Ladies." It had lured half a thousand miners, filling every bench and box. A girl in tight-fitting black trousers was singing, with her forty sisters kicking high behind her. From the boxes came constant pops of champagne corks, each wine girl getting her commission ticket punched with each sale. John Collier, lining up back of the rear bench with five peace officers, saw gold eagles and double eagles tossed on to the stage by a cheering, half-drunken audience. What amazed him was the discipline which kept the girls from scrambling for the coins. "When the number's over," Barry Holden explained, "they'll gather 'em up for a three-way split. Black Pants'll get a third, the house'll get a third, and the forty ladies'll divvy what's left."

What mattered was that Collier failed to see the fake waiter.

A few stops later they looked in at Seth Agnew's Wigwam, an enormous warehouse converted into a sleeping place for overflow drifters. Here they could get a straw mattress for fifty cents the night, the cots crowded so closely that a man had barely room to sit while taking off his boots.

"We're wasting our time here," Gerry Harlan said. "The guy we're lookin' for's too well paid to be in a flop like this."

But Monte Murray disagreed. "Just the place he might pick to hide in. He'd figure we're lookin' for him tonight."

51

"Lots of well-heeled pickpockets sleep here," Barry Holden said, "in order to pick the pockets of sleepers all around them."

Collier was weary in the legs when they left the Wigwam. "One more joint," Tucker promised him, "and we'll call quits for the night."

The place he chose was Pop Jenkins' Concert and Dance Hall on Oak. It featured a Cornish brass band and a gilt sign over the bar said:

IT'S DAY ALL DAY IN THE DAYTIME
AND NO NIGHT IN LEADVILLE

There Tucker's party found faro, keno, poker and roulette at high play, miners and bullwhackers dancing boisterously with underworld women while the chief herder, like a whipcracking ringmaster, kept everything moving.

Pop Jenkins came up, his eyes glassy and his talk oily. "What'll you give me for a tip, gents?" His eyes veered craftily from Tucker to Duggan.

"You've given us tips before," Duggan growled, "and they never pan out."

"What's this one?" Tucker demanded.

Jenkins spread his hands. "I admit it's just bar talk. Happened five or six nights ago. It's about a guy who got shot in an alley. Bryson, the papers called him."

"What about him?"

"Customer said he seen Bryson at a Park Street bar."

"Hold on," Gerry Harlan broke in. "What's the customer's name?"

"They call him Joe," Pop Jenkins said. "That's all I know about him. This Joe said Bryson took the next stool to him, up at a Park Street bar. He pointed to a guy who was just goin' out and asked Joe, 'Who's the stout, heavy-set man with the checkered vest?' "

"Go on," Tucker prodded impatiently.

"Joe said, 'I can't recollect his name right now. But he struck it rich, they claim, on Fryer Hill.' Then Bryson said, 'Looks like a man I knew in California; he killed a man out there and's due for a hangin', if they ever ketch him.' Joe said in a minute Bryson got off his stool and followed the man out."

"Where," Duggan demanded, "can we find Joe?"

Jenkins shrugged. "Search me. He don't come in very often."

"Which Park Street bar was it where he saw Bryson?"

"He didn't say. But there's only one first-class bar on Park. Kelly's Place."

The tip couldn't be ignored. The seven men in Tucker's party hurried to Park Street, a block north of the Clarendon Hotel. The patronage at Kelly's Place was comparatively well dressed and quiet.

Neither Kelly nor his bartender could remember the incident described by Jenkins. "Lots of Joes come in here. And lots of checkered vests. Bryson? I read about him but I never knew him by sight. We don't listen in on bar talk."

Near the rear four men were playing stud poker. A wine girl with a slight figure and a dark Spanish face was filling their glasses. Collier saw Sheriff Tucker's eyes fix with a startled stare on one of the players. "Look, Duggan! Isn't that Wally Welch? The long skinny guy with the handlebar mustaches!"

"Looks like him from the nose up," Duggan said. "Let's take him."

Barry Holden explained to Collier in an undertone. "Welch killed a deputy here a year ago and disappeared. Guess he figures we won't recognize him with those handlebars."

"He's a draw-fighter," Tucker remembered, "and plenty fast. Duggan, you and your boys close in from the left. Rest of us'll take him from the right."

Duggan and his constables loosened their holster guns and advanced three abreast toward the poker table, approaching it from the bar side. Tucker, Harlan and Collier closed in from the wall side. They were still five steps away when Welch looked up and saw them.

Instantly he was on his feet. His left arm circled the wine girl and pinioned her to him. His right hand drew a gun and held it to the girl's back.

As she screamed, the other poker players dived

to the floor and rolled free from any line of fire.

"She gets it," Welch warned, "if you come any closer."

An open door at the bar's rear gave to darkness and he began backing to it, pulling the wine girl with him. Her face blanched under the paint and she screamed again.

Wally Welch backed another step. The girl he dragged with him came only to his neck. His eyes darted back and forth along a line of six armed men—a sheriff, a marshal, a deputy, two constables and a badgeless young stranger. Each of those six had an elbow crooked, poised for a draw yet not daring to risk a shot. The wine girl fainted in Welch's arm-hold as he pulled her another backward step.

"Drop your guns," he commanded, "before I count three. One; two . . ."

Six men each took a gun from its holster and five of those guns dropped to the floor. The sixth one roared in the hand of John Collier and its bullet punched Welch between the eyes.

The man's hold on the girl loosened and she fell forward into Gerry Harlan's arms. Welch reeled sideways, his lanky body jackknifed. His gun went sliding along the floor as the man himself fell heavily across the bar rail.

Duggan stood blinking at a forty-five held by John Collier. "If you can't remember anything," he asked hoarsely, "how did you know you could draw-fight?"

Collier couldn't explain it. He stood sheepish and confused, smoke curling from the muzzle of his gun.

Tucker eyed him shrewdly. "One sure thing— it's not the first time. You've done it before, somewhere, Johnnie Collier."

# Five

Collier slept till nearly noon. When he opened his eyes he saw Gerry Harlan sitting by the bed with his boots propped on Room 278's window sill, looking out at the Harrison Avenue traffic.

The tall deputy looked around with a grin. "You're just in time for the powwow, pardner. Better get your clothes on fast."

Collier swung his legs out of bed. "What powwow?"

"Down in the dining room in half an hour. It's to figure out how to keep you alive till you begin rememberin' things."

"Who all'll be there?"

"Tucker and Duggan for two. Us for two more. The county clerk and his yellow-haired daughter for two more. And a schoolmarm named Lola Loomis."

Collier looked up, blinking. "Where does *she* come in?"

"Search me," Gerry said. "She's a friend of Angela Rand's. Wouldn't mind knowin' her a little better myself. And don't forget to strap on your gun, cowboy. It's still open season on you, indoors and out."

At noon they went fully armed down to the lobby and found five people waiting. Angela presented her father, Milton Rand, a man with prematurely gray hair. His manner toward Collier was stiff, almost hostile. "Frankly I wish my daughter had stayed out of this, Collier. That was a close call she had—up at your tea party."

"Nonsense, Dad," Angela said lightly. "Anyway it wasn't a tea party; it was a coffee party."

"Coffee and arsenic," Milton Rand said severely.

A tall stately brunette a few years older than Angela was presented as Lola Loomis. She held out her hand as her friendly dark eyes met Collier's. "You don't remember me, Mr. Collier?"

"Afraid I don't, Miss Loomis. Maybe you were on the stagecoach with me, when I came to Leadville."

The schoolteacher smiled and shook her head. "I didn't make much of an impression, did I, Angela?"

The seven made an odd party as they went into the dining room—four armed men, a harassed county clerk and two strikingly pretty young girls. The table Tucker had reserved was in a semi-private alcove. As a waitress took their orders Collier wondered who was footing the bill. Especially his own bill. His assailants had stripped him of cash, although luckily he'd paid his room rent a week in advance.

When he asked about it Tucker's answer surprised him. "Seems you've got a backer, Collier. Flint Hammond himself. He keeps a suite of his own here at the Clarendon. When he heard about that gum-shoeing waiter he got mad. Said the same thing might happen to anyone else in the hotel. Told the management to send your bill to him. And if you need anything else, you're to let him know."

"For Flint it's chicken feed," Duggan said. "He's got a silver lining, that fella has."

Rand spoke with a nervous impatience. "Let's get on with it."

"We'll take up Bryson first," Tucker said. "My men have been backtracking him. He arrived here by stage Monday morning. Monday he hung around the hotel, talking to mining men in the lobby and bar, asking about silver production. Said if a bargain turned up he might make an investment.

"Tuesday morning he rode out to Fryer Hill and in the afternoon he rode up Big Strayhorse. Counted carts as they passed by on the way to the smelters. Asked a hundred sharp questions.

Wednesday he covered Breece Hill. Thursday he covered Iron Hill and Carbonate Gulch. If he was interested in any particular property it didn't show in his talk.

"Friday he spent part of the morning looking at two record ledgers in your office, Mr. Rand. Friday afternoon he rode up Little Strayhorse, crossed Breece Hill and disappeared into upmountain timber. Where he went we don't know. That night he wrote two letters and mailed one; before he could mail the other he was shot."

County Clerk Rand reported next. "Bryson used a magnifying glass to look at some entry in Ledger B of the 1879 transfers. The copy clerk who made most of those entries is Raymond Otis. Otis has a small, cramped handwriting in which an 'n' is easily confused with a 'u,' or a capital 'M' with a capital 'W.' A reader might not be sure whether a proper name is, for instance, 'Minter' or 'Winter.' This could apply to any proper name, whether the name of a grantor, a grantee, a mine or an attesting notary. Ledger B has a vast number of such possible confusions; so we can't make an intelligent guess as to which particular name Bryson studied with a reading glass. My opinion is that it's a blind alley as far as the county records are concerned."

A quick disagreement came from his daughter. "I don't think we should give up that easily, Dad."

John Collier eyed her keenly. "You've got an idea or two, maybe?"

"At least two," Angela said. "One is that Mr. Bryson stumbled on a fraud involving a bonanza. Nothing less than a large fortune at stake would make the defrauder resort to murder. You agree, Sheriff?"

Tucker looked at Duggan and both men nodded. "He's not playing for marbles," Duggan muttered.

The girl went on: "Eliminating all entries in Book B which don't involve bonanzas we'd reduce the number to less than a hundred. If from those we pick out the transfers which were notarized at some distant city, we might reduce the number to say ten or fifteen. Then let's write those ten or fifteen grantors asking each if he really made such a transfer as the one recorded."

Six men sat looking at her, none so appreciatively as John Collier. Tucker asked: "You figure maybe a Leadville man forged a non-resident's name to a title and then put the fake title on record?"

"It's a possibility," Angela insisted. "Suppose a claim seemed to be worthless and the owner abandoned it, moving to New York or San Francisco. Then perhaps adjacent strikes make the claim valuable. So a local man forges a transfer from the nonresident to himself and puts it on record. The property goes into bonanza. Then Bryson comes along and stumbles on the truth."

60

Milton Rand gave a half-tolerant smile. "She always did have a vivid imagination," he murmured.

And a face to match it, Collier thought. He looked in growing fascination at the richness of the girl's color and the sparkle of her eyes.

"Some of those grantors," Duggan said, "may had died since they left here."

"Which makes it more possible than ever!" Angela exclaimed. "By forging a dead man's name to a title, the thief would run less risk of being caught." The blue eyes turned alertly to John Collier. "Only the heirs of the defrauded man could ever challenge him. Did a relative of yours ever file a mining claim at Leadville, Mr. Collier?"

He didn't know. And promptly the girl corrected herself. "Really you're Mr. W. Remind me to look in Book B for a nonresident grantor whose mine went into bonanza, and whose name begins with W."

"Now," Tucker said, "let's trace John Collier. He came in on a stage, registered here, asked the clerk what room was occupied by Bryson, was told about Bryson's murder, went up to his room, an hour later came down and left the hotel. Take it from there, Lola."

Lola Loomis fixed her intelligent black eyes on Collier. "You don't remember me, but I was at the corner of Harrison and Jefferson when you tipped your hat and asked where Poplar Street is.

I told you it was a block east. Then you asked how to find the house of a lawyer named Gentry on Poplar Street. I said I was going that way myself and would be glad to point out Mr. Gentry's house. So we walked a block uphill to Poplar. I had on a fetching new bonnet and carried a parasol to match, but alas, you didn't notice. 'Mr. Gentry lives in that green clapboard cottage,' I said, pointing. You thanked me, tipped your hat and went toward it."

Collier's vacant stare changed to a sheepish grin. "How could I forget," he murmured, "a deal like that?"

"I saw you knock at the cottage," Lola said. "Its door opened and you went in. I knew that Mr. Gentry's a bachelor who uses the cottage both for living quarters and a law office. But later I found out that he was in Buena Vista that day. So I reported it to Sheriff Tucker."

"Gentry's a lawyer in good standing," Tucker said. "He never heard of anyone resembling John Collier. Someone who knew he was out of town used his house for a trap. In the back yard we found the tracks of a narrow-tire spring wagon. You were tapped on the head there, Johnnie Collier, then hauled away in a spring wagon. Let's hear from you now, Duggan."

"When the banks opened this morning," the city marshal told them, "Murdy's check for three thousand turned out to be good. The bank says he usually kept only a few dollars in that account; but last Monday he walked in to deposit five thousand in cash. Weekend poker winnings, he claimed."

"More likely a murder payoff," Gerry Harlan snorted. "Bryson was shot Friday night and someone must have paid for the job. Cash, naturally. So the killer couldn't bank it till Monday morning."

"We accepted the bail," Duggan said. "When Murdy left the jail I had him followed. Right now he's holed up with a jug at a rooming house on Oak Street."

A waitress circled the table, passing muffins. Tucker waited till she was gone before taking up the next point. "Bryson," he reminded them, "saw a man in a Park Street bar; a heavy-set man with a rich claim on Fryer Hill and who's wanted in California for murder."

"Which has got nothing to back it up," Duggan derided, "except bar talk from a guy named Joe."

"It's got to be run down," Tucker insisted. "If true, it makes a solid motive for Bryson's murder."

"And for John Colliers," Angela added with a slight shudder, "provided Mr. Bryson wrote him a letter about it."

"The county attorney," Tucker said, "has located three Fryer Hill mining men who fill the bill. They're on the heavy side and their pasts can't be fully accounted for. Names are Ralls, Yeager and

Chandler. All three deny ever having been in California."

"Their property titles are all recorded in Book B," Milton Rand said. "I'll take a good sharp look at those entries."

Angela spoke in an undertone to Collier. "People are taking a good sharp look at you. Since last night you've become a celebrity."

Beyond the alcove's archway the main dining room had midday customers at every table. A hundred eyes were covertly appraising John Collier. Duggan noticed it and grinned dryly. "You can't hardly blame 'em, after that shootin' show you put on at Kelly's Place. Every bar in town's buzzing about you, boy. Some claim you're an outlaw in disguise. Others figure you're a fast-gun lawman from Tombstone."

"But most of us," Tucker hastily amended, "figure you're just a cowboy from parts unknown, saddle-wise and gun-quick like any other range hand. Which reminds me of some advice I just got from Doc Fowler."

"He claims I'm doing fine," Collier said.

"His advice is to put you on a horse, where you belong, instead of corraling you in a hotel room. We're in a race to bring back your memory before somebody guns you down. And accordin' to Fowler the closer you get to your old life, and your old habits, the more likely you'll be to remember where you came from."

"Suits me, Sheriff. When do I start riding?"

"At nine in the morning," Tucker said. "That's when the two men who're watching Murdy have to show up in court as witnesses. So you and Gerry'll relieve them. Follow Murdy no matter where he goes. He might report to whoever paid him the five thousand dollars; or he might join up with Hocker and the fake waiter."

"We'll stick to him like burs," Harlan promised.

"And don't get yourselves shot, please," Angela begged.

"Who's that coming?" Lola Loomis asked.

A man wearing an eyeshade and an alpaca office jacket was advancing across the dining room. He seemed excited and the thing he clutched under his arm looked like a ledger. He burst into the alcove where he met a sharp rebuke from Milton Rand.

"Have you lost your mind, Otis? You know very well those records aren't allowed out of the office!"

The ledger's character was obvious. "LAKE COUNTY LEDGER # B; 1879" was lettered boldly on its ink-stained cover.

Seeing it here shocked Angela no less than her father. It was a book which under no circumstances could be taken beyond the counter; and which at night must be locked in the county clerk's safe.

"He had on an overcoat and a droopy-brim hat,"

the copy clerk reported. "A short stocky man with a spade beard. Asked to see Ledger B and I put it on the counter for him. When he got through looking at it he shoved it back to me. I thought it was the same book. . . ."

Milton Rand snatched the ledger and whipped it open. "The real book's gone," Otis mourned. "Under his overcoat, I guess, when he went out."

They all stared at the blank pages. This book had no entries whatever.

# Six

Keeping Murdy in sight, Gerry Harlan and John Collier rode cautiously out Jefferson Street, east toward Fryer Hill. Each man had a carbine in his saddle scabbard and a holster gun on his thigh. Dust clouds hung from innumerable ore carts which passed them, the loaded ones moving downhill toward the smelters, the empties returning uphill to the mines. It was ten in the morning and an hour ago Harlan and Collier had relieved the two officers who'd been watching an Oak Street rooming house.

Almost at once Murdy, after picking up a livery horse, had ridden leisurely out of town. His tailers kept well behind him, hat brims low and collars turned high. "The dust'll help hide us," Gerry said.

"He doesn't seem to be in a hurry. Who's that he's talking to?"

"Looks like he's bumming a smoke from a cart driver."

Two mine-pocked gulches came together at the east end of Jefferson and each had a wagon trail. "That's Little Strayhorse Gulch to the right," Gerry said. "Its road leads to Mosquito Pass and End-of-Track. Other gulch is Big Strayhorse. The mines up it are gettin' a big play right now."

They stopped, waiting for Murdy to ride on. "If he takes the Mosquito Pass road he may figure to jump bail and leave the county."

"Where does the other gulch go, Gerry?"

"To a high wild country up toward Ten Mile. From the head of it you could go on over the divide to Georgetown."

As far as one could see the mountainside was splotched with ore dumps. A constant rumble of discords came from tipples as ore was poured into wagons and carts. Many of the claims had wire fences; others were enclosed in stout pole stockades to keep out high-graders. The claims had been rudely or carelessly surveyed and many a claim overlapped its neighbors. Each claim was fifteen hundred feet long by three hundred feet wide.

Yesterday Collier and Harlan had walked Angela and Lola to Angela's house, after lunch at the Clarendon, and on the way Angela had thumbnailed the district's brief history. "In the last twenty months," she'd told them, "thirty thousand mining claims have been filed. Lots of them are being jumped and fought over and disputed in court; no one feels safe till his claim's proved, patented and recorded."

Collier licked a cigaret and thought of a stolen ledger book. "It'll start a panic, won't it, Gerry, when people find out what happened to Book B?"

Harlan nodded. "That's why Milt Rand wants to keep it a secret, long as possible." So far only yesterday's luncheon party and Rand's staff knew about the stolen ledger. People coming in to look at it would be told that it had been sent to a bindery to be rebound. "It'll stave off a riot for a few days, maybe."

"And after that?"

"*Quien sabe*? In the long run it won't hurt honest titles. Each owner's got his deed or patent on file at home. If there's nothing phony about it, he can always take it back to the county clerk and have it recorded in another book."

Ahead of them, Murdy was riding on. But at the fork of Big and Little Strayhorse gulches he took neither; instead he rode straight up a slope to the brow of Fryer Hill. Harlan and Collier followed, screened by dust. "He's stopped again," Collier said presently.

Murdy had reined up at the gate of a stockaded claim and was talking to the guard there. Ore loads were streaming out through the gate, smelter-bound. "It's the *Little Pittsburgh*," Gerry said. "Richest mine on the hill."

Angela had told Collier about it. In May of last year Haw Tabor had grubstaked a German shoemaker named Rische. Rische had struck mineral at a shallow depth and a few months later had sold out to his grubstaker for three hundred thousand dollars. Since then Tabor had taken more than a million in silver from this one mine.

"And he's got plenty of others," Harlan said. "The *Matchless* is his pet."

Murdy was riding on again and they followed, Gerry occasionally pointing out one of the big producers. "That's Colonel Titus' *Shamrock* over there, Johnnie. See that brass cannon at the gate? And those armed guards? The *Shamrock*'s been jumped three times and seven men have been killed in a title fight."

"Who's Murdy talking to now, Gerry?"

"Looks like Red Buford. Red's George Yeager's foreman at the *Aztec*. Man was found dead at the bottom of the *Aztec* shaft last month. Accident, maybe; or maybe he was pushed in. It's happened before, up here on Fryer Hill. A ton of solid silver per day makes plenty to squabble over."

Murdy led them down into Big Strayhorse and past the *Morning Star*, a bonanza property of Flint Hammond. From there he rode east and northeast to Breece Hill. "Seems to be lookin' for someone," Gerry said, "the way he's zigzaggin'."

Here they were out of the bonanza district and ore carts were fewer. Occasionally they passed a shut-down mine, like the *Lost Chance* on Victoria Hill and the *Evening Star* on Breece.

A gulch cut through an upper corner of Breece Hill and a cluster of shacks there included a store-saloon. In early afternoon Murdy stopped to eat there. The two who followed waited out of sight till he rode on.

"I could use a beer myself," Harlan said.

The storeman served them. "Was that Herb Murdy who just passed here?" Gerry asked.

"He didn't say."

"Ever see him before?"

"Nope."

"Did he say where he's going?"

"Nope. But he asked if Rufe Small's at home. I said I ain't seen Rufe since last spring."

"Thanks." Harlan and Collier rode on.

A mile or so upmountain they saw Murdy disappear into pine timber. "If he's heading for Rufe Small's cabin," Gerry said, "we don't need to keep him in sight any longer."

"Who's Rufe Small?"

"Traps fur in winter and hunts meat summer and fall. Peddles venison to miners and sometimes sells 'em a bearskin robe."

"Is he on the level?"

"I'd bet on it, Johnnie."

They rode on to the tree line and picked up Murdy's tracks. "He's heading toward Rufe's cabin," Harlan concluded.

The hoof marks led them to a high steep canyon with a dense growth of conifers on either side. "We're better'n eleven thousand feet elevation," Harlan said. "Good bear country up here. Come to think of it, it was right about here that Chick Croddy shot that grizzly he stuffed and set in front of his shop."

"Lucky for me he did," Collier said. The word made him rein to a stop. "Speaking of luck, Gerry, aren't we having a little too much of it? I mean isn't this just a little too easy?"

The senior deputy chewed on it a moment, then nodded shrewdly. "You're dead right, pardner; it's a sight too easy. Him ridin' slow, with plenty of stops to make sure we don't lose him. Then asking that come-on question about Rufe Small. Could be he's luring us on."

"Smack into an ambush, Gerry." Collier looked thoughtfully up the narrow, shallow canyon, with its screen of trees on either side.

"We'd be ducks, Johnnie, for a couple of repeating rifles."

"We wouldn't know what hit us," Collier agreed.

"It's *you* they want, Johnnie. As long as Pete and Sam were watching Murdy, he didn't leave his rooming house. But quick as you and I took over, he lit out for the hills. He's leading us to the slaughter like a pair of fat steers."

"How far to the cabin?"

"Couple of miles. From here on we'd better keep under cover."

They got into the trees on the left side of the canyon. Here there was no trail and the going was slow. Presently Gerry said, "We'll do better afoot, Johnnie."

After tying their mounts they took their rifles and moved on afoot, keeping parallel with the canyon. Slowly and quietly they advanced, watching the ravine's rim for ambushers hiding there. The only life they flushed was a doe with fawn by her side. "Maybe we guessed wrong, Johnnie."

"Or maybe they're holed up in the cabin, Gerry, waiting for us to walk in."

A mile farther on they sighted the cabin and it seemed deserted. "We'll circle to the back," Harlan said.

Trees hid them until they were above and back of the cabin. The place still looked lifeless. It had rough log walls and a sod roof. There was no sign that horses had been near it recently.

Firewood stacked on the upper side had clearly been there for many months. Harlan, his gun out and cocked, advanced to the back door and pushed it open. The single room had a musty smell and there was no occupant.

They went in and knew at once that Rufe Small was absent for the season. His bedroll and clothing were gone. Winter traps hung from pegs but the shelves had no food on them. "He won't be back till fur season," Harlan said.

"Does he wear glasses?" Collier asked.

"Not Rufe Small. He's got the eyes of an Indian. Why?"

"Someone who's been here wears glasses." Collier picked up a spectacles case made to be carried in a pocket.

"Better keep it, Johnnie," Gerry decided. "If we run onto anyone who's mislaid a specs case we'll ask what the heck he was doing here."

The ambush theory still looked good. For since Murdy had headed for this cabin and hadn't arrived, he must have stopped in the canyon below here. He could have met friends and be waiting with them to waylay Harlan and Collier.

"Maybe we took the wrong side, coming up," Gerry concluded. "We'll take the opposite side going back."

They left the shack and again got into timber. Again they moved silently through the forest, paralleling the ravine on the side opposite to the route of approach. After half a mile Gerry nudged Collier. "Careful! See those big gray boulders ahead of us? They'd make a right good place for drygulchers. We'll sneak up for a look."

The look, a minute later, showed them the backs

of three men. They were crouched behind the rocks with rifles aimed at the canyon trail.

"The middle one's Murdy," Gerry whispered.

The two other ambushers couldn't be seen frontally. One was burly, the other slim. The fake waiter, Collier remembered, had been of slim build. On a guess the third man could be Hocker who'd escaped from the runaway-mules wreck.

Their horses weren't in sight. It was clear that they were expecting an approach from down-canyon.

Ten paces from them Gerry signaled for a stop. "We'll keep 'em covered," he whispered, "and wait for 'em to talk. Maybe they'll give us a tip-off."

John Collier took an aim on the middle man and waited. A restless minute went by, then a growl of impatience from the man on the right. "Looks like they turned back, Murdy."

"Keep your shirt on, Gil," Murdy said. "They wouldn't dog me this far without comin' all the way."

Another silent wait while Collier felt the sweating suspense of it cool his cheek. Then the leftmost man said: "Gives me the creeps, waitin' like this. Like holdin' a bag fer snipe."

"You're gettin' paid fer it, ain'tcha?" Murdy retorted. "The boss ain't stingy, neither."

"He dassent be," Gil said. "He's a gone goose if he lets that cowboy remember who he is."

"And all because you let a pair of snaky mules

run away with you! We could've had our dough and been in Frisco by this time."

Another wait but no more talk came with it. A squirrel scolded from a pine limb and John Collier, shifting his weight to the other leg, crackled a twig under his boot.

The sound alerted Murdy. "What was that? I heard something!"

"You heard *us*." Gerry Harlan stood up to his full six-feet-three, rifle stock to cheek with a steady aim on Gil Hocker. "Drop your guns and elevate your paws, all of you."

The ambushers froze, still gripping their rifles. "I'd a heap rather take you in alive," Gerry said. "But if you'd rather shoot it out, go ahead."

A clatter was Murdy dropping his rifle. The outside men whirled, firing. John Collier shifted his aim to the fake waiter and fired, saw the man double forward. Harlan squeezed his trigger twice and made two hits; but still Hocker kept shooting. He remained on his knees, livid and stubborn, till he'd emptied his magazine; but a bullet in the stomach made his shots go wild.

"I give up! Don't shoot!" The cry came from Murdy whose back was still this way. His arms hid his face as he pleaded for his life.

Gerry Harlan collared him, shoved him face down between two dead men. "He's stinking scared, Johnnie, so maybe he'll talk. I'll see what I can get out of him while you bring up the horses."

# Seven

The five horses filed in tandem downcanyon with Harlan leading the three outlaw mounts and with Collier bringing up the rear. Murdy, roped to his saddle, was still in a pasty funk but had given out no information likely to be the truth.

The other two saddles carried dead men—Gil Hocker and the thin, wiry man who'd posed as a waiter at the Clarendon.

Harlan turned in his saddle for another look. "He's Harry the Tipper, all right. Used to be assistant night barkeep at the Grand Hotel. Means we're up against the Gus Culp gang. We ran 'em outa Leadville last spring, but it looks like they're back."

They stopped at the Breece Gulch store to borrow two wagon sheets and cover the dead men. Miners at the bar there came out to make a gaping circle around the five horses. "What the heck did they do, Gerry?"

"Show up in court when we try Murdy," Gerry said, "and you'll find out."

Beyond the store there was a cart road with room to ride abreast. Collier rode stirrup to stirrup with Harlan, the captive mounts strung along behind. "The Gus Culp gang?" Collier prompted.

"They terrorized Leadville all last winter and spring," Gerry said. "An organized gang of footpads and dark-of-the-moon garroters. They always knew where the fat wallets were. When we broke it up they left this county and took to robbing Barlow and Sanderson stages on the Canon City run. Then Gus Culp took a bullet in the leg and the whole gang moved to Arizona." Gerry thumbed toward a canvas bulge on one of the horses. "Harry the Tipper was one of them."

"He worked at the Grand Hotel?"

"That's right. The Clarendon didn't open till a month or so ago. The leading hotel was the Grand on Chestnut. Most of the big silver men did their drinking at the Grand bar. They used to have a lot of high-stake poker games in a cardroom off that bar. Harry the assistant night barkeep carried drinks to 'em. It gave Harry a chance to spot the big winner. Five times in three months the big winner was stopped on his way home, on a dark street at two or three in the morning, garroted and robbed. None of the other players was ever bothered."

"Means the footpads were always tipped off by Harry."

"Sure, Johnnie. But we didn't dope it out till it happened five times. The sixth time we followed the big winner home and saw seven thugs jump him the minute he hit a dark street. There was a gun battle with one constable and one thug killed.

The rest got away but not before we recognized the leader, Gus Culp."

"And Harry?"

"For a while he stuck to his post at the Grand bar and there was no way to prove he'd really tipped them. Then he quit and disappeared. Next seen he was one of a gang of stage robbers who held up a coach near Salida. They did a dozen more stage jobs before a leg wound made Culp pull out for Arizona."

"They're taking a big chance, looks like, coming back to Leadville."

"All outlaws take big chances, Johnnie. Usually they'll go where the biggest money is. Right now the biggest money's here in Leadville."

"Stagecoach money?"

"Blood money, wherever they can get it. Looks like it's *your* blood they're after, pardner. Whoever wants you dead has made a deal with them."

It was sundown when they crossed the bonanza district of Fryer Hill. There a number of cart drivers stopped them to ask questions. Riders circled about Harlan's party when it became known that two of the saddles carried dead men.

There were mutterings and lynch talk by the time they struck the head of Jefferson Street. A growing uninvited escort glared at a prisoner roped to his saddle. "Is this the bugger who poisoned Cal Barstow?"

"He's Murdy," Gerry said. "The phony waiter's

dead. You couldn't make him any deader by hangin' him."

"Can't see what difference it makes," a mucker growled. "One's as bad as the other. The whole caboodle orter be strung up."

"They'll be strung up legal," Gerry predicted. In view of the crowd's temper he didn't mention his conclusion that Murdy and both the dead men had been part of the Gus Culp gang of garroting footpads.

At the county jail Tucker and his jailer came out to meet them. The jailer took charge of Murdy and then Deputy Pete Loftus appeared to take over the dead men. "Pass 'em on to the coroner, Pete," Tucker said.

He listened to Harlan's report. "You boys had a pretty busy day! Humph! So you figure Gus Culp's back in town, eh, Gerry?"

"That's my hunch, Sheriff. Him and his whole outfit of stranglers."

"There's a reason to think you're right." With a gleam in his eye the sheriff added: "A better reason than you think. But I'll let Angela Rand tell you about it at supper."

John Collier gave him a blank look. "Supper? Where?"

"At the Rand house on the hill." Tucker grinned impishly. "I forgot to tell you. Angela just sent an invite to both of you. That good-lookin' school-marm'll be there too, Gerry. Seems those gals dug up something today and they want to let you in on it."

"Let's go wash up, Johnnie," Harlan said.

"Keep your guns on, party or no party," the sheriff cautioned. "And stick together, you boys, day and night."

It was dark by the time they'd made themselves presentable and climbed Capitol Hill to the Rand residence, which was directly across from August Meyer's imposing three-story mansion. Angela, in a low-cut evening dress with a barrel skirt, met them at the door.

"Did the sheriff tell you?" she asked excitedly.

"He saved it for you," Collier said. "What's the secret?"

"We found out who stole the ledger," the girl told them.

They joined Lola Loomis in the parlor. Then Milton Rand came in looking dourly disturbed. "I've posted guards front and back," he said. "Dash it, Angela, I've a mind to put you on a stagecoach tomorrow and send you to Denver for a month. You'll get yourself shot if you stay here and keep playing detective."

"Be sensible, Dad," Angela protested. "If those men wanted to shoot me they could follow me to Denver; or hold up my stage on the way there."

"What's it all about?" Collier asked blankly.

A Negro servant announced supper and they

went into a dining room. When they were seated Angela said, "Please calm down, Dad, and ask the blessing."

In no mood for it, Milton Rand bowed his head and mumbled.

Through a moonlit window Collier saw a rifle-armed constable standing guard. "Why would they bother you, Angela?"

"Because she's too blamed smart," her father said, "for her own good."

The girl quickly explained. "Today Lola and I went to the office and questioned Raymond Otis. He's the copy clerk who told us about the stolen ledger. We asked him to describe the man again."

"Did he hand out anything new?"

"No. A bearded man with a stocky build, he said, wearing an overcoat and a droopy-brim hat. That's all he noticed. But Lola and I went out into the hall and found a porter who'd been sweeping there at about the time the book was stolen. He remembers the overcoated man. He says the man hurried as he went out to his horse. The hurry made him limp a little, favoring his left leg."

Gerry Harlan banged a fist into his palm. "Did you hear that, Johnnie? The left leg was where Gus Culp took a bullet, the last time he robbed a Canon City stage. And look, ladies! We bumped into some pals of his today, up the mountain."

When he told them about an ambush in a high-country canyon, there could be little doubt left.

At least two of the three ambushers had been members of the Culp gang which had terrorized Leadville last winter and spring. And yesterday's ledger thief, limping to his horse, must have been Culp himself.

All through the meal Milton Rand fretted about danger to Angela. "They'll stop at nothing, those devils! They'd as lief kill you as look at you!"

"But why me, Dad?"

"Because it was you," Rand argued, "who told us about Bryson coming in to look at the records. It was you who suggested writing letters to all nonresident grantors in Book B, in cases where the transferred property has gone into big money. And it was you who spotted the ledger thief as a limper named Culp. Except for you there'd be no reason to connect Bryson's death with a title fraud, or with Gus Culp. Culp won't thank you for it."

Neither would the man higher up, Collier thought, who was hiring Culp's guns.

After supper Milton Rand went into his study, leaving the young people in the parlor. A stringed instrument in the corner caught Collier's attention and he asked idly, "Who plays the guitar?"

"Dad used to," Angela said, "when he was young and gay." An afterthought made her look curiously at her guest. "How can you know it's a guitar? It must be the first one you've seen since losing your memory."

"That's right. How can I?" Collier picked up the guitar and struck a chord. "Golly! It's a mile out of tune."

Mechanically his fingers began tuning it. The next minute he was strumming melodious chords.

"How on earth can you do it?" Angela wondered. "But since you can, Lola has a lovely voice. Sing 'Juanita,' Lola."

Lola sang a verse of the old Spanish song while John Collier chorded for her. "I just don't know how or why," he murmured.

Apparently the amnesia didn't obstruct or handicap his physical skills. These were entrenched in him and automatic. Horsemanship, a fast gundraw, plucking a guitar—all were a familiar part of him which didn't need the guidance of a mental memory.

"How long," Lola wondered, "do you think we can keep the secret of the stolen ledger?"

Angela's quick answer surprised them all. "I think the wrong people know about it already. They've got spies in the public offices. Think a minute. What was the best time for Culp to steal the ledger? Obviously while Dad and I were attending a conference at the Clarendon. They couldn't have known that unless someone at the county or city offices tipped them off. Next, how did they know Gerry Harlan and John Collier would relieve the guards watching Murdy's rooming house? An insider must have told them.

Otherwise there'd have been no time to arrange an ambush."

Lola looked horrified. "You mean we have criminals right in the city hall?"

"Of course we have," Angela insisted. "What can you expect of a government run partly by the fee system and partly by the fine-and-license system? That's why I'm begging Dad to get out of it and take a job in a bank."

A sober look on Harlan's face meant that he knew it was true. "Lots of apples in the barrel are rotten," he admitted. "Hardly a week passes that Duggan doesn't have to fire a constable for splitting loot with some footpad. Tucker's staff won't assay much higher. For a split they'll look the other way while bunco men fleece a sucker. Everybody knows what goes on in the assessor's office. If some big property owner wants his assessment cut in half, he just slips fifty dollars to some crooked deputy assessor. The *Chronicle* claims it'll always be that way till we change to the salary system."

"The city force is the worst," Angela said. "They get fat off bribery and kickbacks. That's why the Culp gang could be so bold last winter and spring—and why they're not afraid to come back now." The girl looked at the holstered guns worn by two of her guests as though the very fact of them proved her point. Only in Leadville would two young men need guns in order to walk a few blocks to a supper party.

When it was over the girls went out to the front walk with them. Lola was spending the night with Angela. Across the street all three floors of the tall, square Meyer house were lighted. Piano music and gay laughter meant that a party was going on there too. "I saw them arrive," Angela said. "All the big mine owners—Tabor, Fryer, Tom Berdell, Vic Werner, Flint Hammond."

Harlan chuckled. "August Meyer's the only smart one in the bunch. He lets them dig the ore while he refines it for 'em. Makes a profit off every ton they haul to his smelter without taking any risk himself."

"There's a hack over in front of the Meyer house," Angela said. "You'll be safer riding home in it."

"We're not *that* scared," Gerry said. "Come along, Johnnie."

They walked down a short steep hill to the head of Harrison. Taking the west side of it their boots crunched on gravel until they came to Seventh Street, where the board sidewalk began.

This was the decent end of town, residential and saloonless. At Seventh three of the corners had stores, dark and locked for the night. A log dwelling on the fourth corner had a stone chimney on the Seventh Street side and a dark, open window facing Harrison.

The rifle shot which cracked from that window

made Collier's hat tip back on his head. Gerry's tug at his coat pulled him to a crouch on the walk. "I saw the flash. Stay low, Johnnie."

Squatting on his heels, Harlan drew his forty-five and sent four shots across Harrison to the log dwelling's window. Collier followed with two shots of his own. They heard glass shatter over there.

When no return fire came Gerry said, "Let's take him." He walked swiftly across the street, reloading as he advanced, Collier keeping elbow to elbow. From a block down Harrison came a constable's whistle and they could hear men running this way. "How far did he miss you, Johnnie?"

"How did he know I'd be coming along?" Collier wondered. He broke into a run and reached the porch first. There he kicked at a door and found it locked.

"He'll be ducking out the back way," Gerry guessed.

They circled to the rear where moonlight showed an open back door. In the distance up an alley they could hear a retreating runner. If the sniper had been alone here the house would now be empty.

"Let's make sure, Johnnie." They went into a dark kitchen and struck a match. It brought no challenge. The kitchen table had an oil lamp and Harlan lighted it. A single glass half full of stale beer suggested that the sniper had waited alone here.

Clearly he'd known about the supper date at the Rand House. Returning from it, John Collier would need to pass here. "They're in a sweat to snuff you out, Johnnie, before you begin rememberin' things."

They went into a front room, taking the lamp with them. From the floor below a bullet-smashed street window Gerry picked up an empty rifle shell. "Your ticket to Kingdom Come, Johnnie; only he missed."

"Angela was right," Collier said, "about a leak at the city hall or courthouse." For surely someone down there had tipped off the sniper about a date with two girls on Capitol Hill.

"What's that you're fishin' out of the fireplace, Johnnie?"

An odd odor had drawn Collier to the parlor fireplace. With a pair of tongs he began picking charred fragments from the ashes there. They were from the cover of a large, cloth-bound book, he concluded. "Right here, Gerry, is where they burned Ledger B."

# Eight

It was a half hour before midnight when a sleek, ruddy young man crossed the Clarendon lobby and spoke with a breezy confidence to the night clerk. "Has Mr. Hammond gone up yet?"

"Do you have an appointment, Mr. Janford?" the clerk asked.

"I'm a little late for it," Melville Janford evaded. "If he's turned in I'll come back in the morning."

Flint Hammond was a man of vast affairs, and to the night clerk it didn't seem strange that a lawyer would be calling on him even at this late hour. Although specializing in title cases, Janford was also known to be a fixer who could pull deft strings around the city and county offices. Upon occasion many of the more important mine owners, including H. A. W. Tabor himself, had found him useful.

The lawyer skipped up to the second floor and turned down the south wing, the far four rooms of which comprised the private suite of Flint Hammond. Over its entrance door hung a silver horseshoe forged from the first ingot ever produced from Hammond's fabulous *Morning Star* mine.

A sardonic smile curved Janford's lips as he

looked up at the horseshoe. Then he knocked and the door was opened by a dark, half-bald Italian who acted both as valet and errand runner for Hammond.

"Is he still up, Lippo?"

Lippo, a swart, quiet man wearing thick-lensed glasses, nodded toward an inner room which the silver king used as a home office and where most of his more intimate affairs were transacted. This larger sitting room was furnished for the entertainment of guests, for Flint Hammond often had informal parties here.

A third compartment of the suite was a master bedroom, while a fourth held kitchen equipment, a liquor cabinet and a cot for Lippo.

Janford crossed to the office and entered without knocking. Hammond, still in the dinner jacket he'd worn at August Meyer's house earlier tonight, sat at a desk with a tangle of papers before him.

He looked up half bitterly when he saw the lawyer. "Never mind the bad news, Janford. I've already heard it. Buckshot missed."

"Yeh, I figured you'd know that. It's all over town." Like a man sure of himself and bent on proving it with a degree of impudence, the lawyer sat down and hoisted his feet to the desk. "But that's not what I came to tell you."

Hammond gave him a startled look. "You mean they've caught Buckshot?"

"No. When he missed he beat it out the back

way and made off up an alley. All the same I've got some bad news, Flint."

Hammond frowned. Being called Flint by a shyster like Janford always annoyed him. "I'm fed up with bad news," he snapped. "What is it this time?"

Janford leaned forward and lowered his voice. "You know the canyon ambush went sour, I suppose?"

"Who doesn't? What with Warren and Harlan parading into town with two dead men and a prisoner!"

"Better not call him Warren," the lawyer advised. "Call him Collier like everyone else does. If you get used to calling him Warren, you might make a slip in public."

"Come to the point, Janford."

Lippo came in with highballs and set them on the desk. Then silently he withdrew, although Hammond had no secrets from Lippo.

"Two dead men and Murdy," Janford said, "isn't all they brought in. They brought in a spectacles case and left it at the sheriff's office. They'll show it to the local eye doctors and tomorrow they hope to find out who prescribed the glasses which match that case."

The peril of it struck Hammond at once and drained some of the rich, wine-red color from his face. "You mean Lippo's glasses case? Where did they pick it up?"

"At the trapper's cabin. Lippo must have left it there when he made a night ride to set things up."

Hammond swore under his breath. "Damn Lippo!"

"It'll draw an inquiry right to your door, Flint."

"It won't prove anything."

"Sure it won't. But you can't afford to have attention swing your way. As long as you're not remotely suspected you're safe. But the minute you are, people will begin wondering if it wasn't *your* title to the *Morning Star* that Bryson was looking at with a reading glass." The lawyer's eyes shifted to a steel safe where the title itself was now stored. "If Bryson had been looking at the original transfer paper, instead of merely at a copy in the county clerk's ledger, he'd have seen that you'd rubbed out *'Eve'* and substituted *'Mor.'* Which changed *Evening Star,* a borderline property now shut down, into *Morning Star* which is making you rich by the minute."

"Job Norcross is dead," Hammond reminded him.

"Yes, but the Kansas City notary who notarized his signature isn't. The name of that notary public shows on both your copy and the recorded copy. If questioned by mail, he'd remember that the mine transferred was *not* the *Morning Star,* but the *Evening Star.* That smart little Rand girl was planning to send out letters to all names connected with transfers from nonresident owners, in cases involving a bonanza. One of those letters would have gone to a Kansas City notary."

Hammond didn't need to be told about it. Sensing the danger himself he'd given orders for Ledger B to be stolen and burned. His own title couldn't be challenged, because the original instrument was locked in his safe. But if his personal servant should be identified as the client for whom a certain pair of glasses had been provided, a spotlight would at once be turned on Lippo's master, and upon the *Morning Star* mine.

Flint Hammond drank angrily from his highball, then called Lippo from the kitchen.

When the Italian came he slapped a hard hand on the man's mouth. "You bungling fool! After all our trouble and risk of covering up, you have to lose your glasses case at that cabin!" With the flat of his hand he struck again and left a livid streak on the servant's cheek.

"I am sorry," Lippo said. "I do not miss it till I am back in town."

"Get out of my sight before I break your neck!"

"Yes, *maestro*." Lippo bowed himself out. He had good reason never to leave Flint Hammond, no matter how badly he was treated.

Melville Janford's face showed a cynical smile. "You'd like to break *my* neck too! You'd have done it two months ago if you'd dared—ever since I tapped you for a cut. That's why I sent to Arizona for the Culp outfit—and cut them in on it too. Putting me out of the way wouldn't do you any good now. Besides, there's enough for all of us. And we can leave the strong-arming to Culp."

"And the pussyfooting to you!" Hammond added bitterly.

"Why not? I know all the angles down at the city and county offices, don't I? I know who'll take a bribe and who won't. That's how I was able to pick up this specs case." Janford brought the missing case from his pocket and tossed it on the desk. "Proves I'm earning my cut, don't it? Give it back to Lippo."

Hammond gaped at the case. It was Lippo's all right. "How the devil did you get it?"

"By knowing that the property clerk in Tucker's office has an itchy palm. He keeps the stuff they take off prisoners, along with odd clews, in a locked drawer. I gave him fifty dollars to slip me the specs case."

"He'll keep his mouth shut?"

"He'd better. Before he was a property clerk, he was a bribe-taking deputy assessor."

Relief relaxed Hammond. "Maybe I've under-estimated you, Janford."

"I missed out on one bet, though," the lawyer admitted as he licked a cigaret. "Twice I tried to date the Rand girl. Thought maybe I could get some inside info on what goes on in her old man's office."

"And she turned you down?"

"Cold." The lawyer grimaced wryly. "But young War— I mean young Collier's having better luck. They're gettin' chummy, those two. Which is something to keep in mind, Flint."

"The main thing to keep in mind," Hammond snapped, "is that he may get his memory back any day or hour. If he does, he'll know who he is and why he came here. He'll remember what was in the letter he got from Bryson."

Janford agreed briskly. "Truest thing you ever said, Flint. I'll tell Culp you've doubled the price on him. Okay?"

Hammond nodded grudgingly. "But only if it happens before he starts remembering. As long as he stays alive we're sitting on dynamite."

Janford blandly corrected him. "You mean *you're* sitting on dynamite. There's no *phony* title recorded in my name; or any forged deed in my safe. In a bust-up I'll claim I'm just an attorney you came to for advice. Which reminds me—" He held out a hand, open palm up. "Let's have that fifty I had to cough up at the sheriff's office."

Hammond took fifty dollars from his wallet and slammed it in the hand. "Now get out of here, you two-timing shyster! The sight of you makes me sick!"

When the lawyer was gone Flint Hammond sipped his highball somberly, reviewing the last devious months of his life. Fortune was rolling his way but the taste of it was turning sour in his mouth. Half that fortune would have been more than he could spend—but in a sudden swift beckoning of greed he'd snatched for the other half, Job Norcross' half, and now it was too late to change his course. He had a bear by the tail and couldn't let go. Treachery and murder lay heavy on his backtrack. Leeches like Janford and Culp had fastened on him. Now all he could do was cover up and keep raking in what rightfully belonged to Job Norcross' nephew and only heir, Wesley Warren.

At the outset it had seemed so simple and riskless. He thought back to the time nineteen months ago when he and Job Norcross had staked out the *Morning Star* claim in Big Strayhorse Gulch. At that time this was only a wildcat camp called Oro, without any rich strikes, and when fewer than a dozen cabins lined the gulch which later became Leadville. After sinking a shaft sixty feet deep they'd found only enough pay-rock to make the filing patentable; not enough to tempt further digging. So after applying for a patent they'd moved to what later became Breece Hill and there had filed a second claim, the *Evening Star.*

The *Evening Star* made a better showing. It was bringing them about twenty dollars a day when Norcross, much older than Hammond and less rugged, found that his heart wouldn't stand the high altitude. He'd leased his half of the *Evening Star* to Hammond and gone back to Missouri. During the rest of 1878 Hammond had worked the *Evening Star* alone, making a bare living out of it after sending a fourth of his net in cash to Norcross in Kansas City.

"I wish it was still that way!" The words came audibly from Hammond and he meant them. He downed the rest of his liquor and tamped tobacco in his pipe. A pipe usually made him relax but tonight it didn't. The hazard of Wesley Warren pressed like a damp blanket on his brain.

It was in January of '79, just seven months ago, that he received a letter from Job Norcross saying that medical and hospital bills made it necessary for him to raise a thousand dollars, and offering to sell his half of the *Evening Star* for that sum. No mention was made of the *Morning Star,* since at that time it had never produced anything and was considered worthless. The offer was a fair one. So on a standard printed transfer form Hammond had filled in the name *Evening Star,* describing it as a mining claim filed by Flint Hammond and Job Norcross and patented on a certain date, as duly recorded in the records of Lake County, Colorado. He'd clipped his check for a thousand dollars to the paper and mailed it to Norcross. Back had come the title, properly signed and notarized, making Flint Hammond sole owner of the *Evening Star.*

It left him still joint owner with Norcross in the *Morning Star* in Big Strayhorse Gulch. That patent was also recorded in a Lake County ledger. But since it had never earned them a penny, both Hammond and Norcross had all but forgotten it.

Then, before Flint Hammond had taken time to put his new deed on record, word had come of Job Norcross' death. That same week the operators of the *Winter Queen,* adjoining the *Morning Star,* had struck rich ore at seventy feet.

The *Morning Star* shaft was only sixty feet deep. Eagerly Hammond had sent a crew there to deepen that shaft—and at seventy feet had struck a ledge of ore assaying seven hundred ounces of silver to the ton.

His first thought—what a shame he hadn't bought half the *Morning Star* from Norcross instead of half the *Evening Star!* But Norcross was now dead. So why not rub out the *Eve* and substitute *Mor?* It would be equally simple to change a date of patent.

The tug of avarice had been irresistible. The copy clerk at the county office where the transfer was copied into Book B hadn't noticed the erasure. He wasn't likely to in the rush of the boom nor did he even know that the *Morning Star* was about to become a bonanza. And presently the rigged title paper was returned to Hammond and stored under lock with his private papers.

For eight months now the *Morning Star* had

produced thirty tons of ore a day averaging four hundred ounces of silver to the ton. After paying mining, hauling and smelter charges Hammond's daily net from the mine was running close to five thousand dollars. The vein could easily hold up for another year or so; always providing that Hammond could continue hiding the fraud.

How a tricky lawyer had ferreted out the truth Hammond didn't know. Janford, playing cat-and-mouse, had never told him. He'd simply come to Hammond two months ago with a blunt demand for two per cent of the *Morning Star* net. "And another two per cent for a crew of strong-armers I've got back of me, just to make sure you don't hire someone to cut my throat. Far as that goes, we'll earn every cent of our split; you'll needmy brains and Culp's guns before you're through cashing in, Flint Hammond."

In all his frustrated fury at them Hammond was forced to admit that they *had* earned their split. Without them Frank Bryson would have scuttled him. Those two letters Bryson had written, one to Wesley Warren on a Nebraska ranch, the other to a notary in Kansas City, told the whole story. The one to the Missouri notary, still unmailed, had been taken from Bryson's body. The one to young Warren had been taken from his pocket in a Poplar Street cottage, just before Hocker had hauled him away in a spring wagon. Except for a stuffed bear on Chestnut

Street, Wesley Warren would now be rotting at the bottom of the Arkansas River.

So all in all Hammond's unwelcome allies had earned their divvies. A spectacles case on the desk proved it. He pressed a buzzer to summon Lippo.

Lippo came in and the bruise on his face brought a grudging apology from Hammond. "I'm sorry, Lippo. But you shouldn't be so careless. No harm done this time. We found your glasses case. After this don't leave it in the wrong place."

"I deserve that you punish me," Lippo said humbly. "Never will it happen again."

"It better not," Hammond warned. "We don't want sheriffs knocking at our door. If they'd traced this case to you, they'd 've come straight here with questions."

"I do not like sheriffs with questions, *maestro*."

"I should think you wouldn't. Remember you're wanted in Italy and that both you and Marta came here with forged passports. By the way, would you like to send for Marta?"

The Latin face lighted up. "That I wish more than all things, please." Marta, Lippo's wife, was working in a restaurant at Pueblo. She could not be conveniently housed in this bachelor suite of Hammond's at a Leadville hotel.

"Now I have use for her, Lippo. So you may write her a letter and tell her—Hold on; did I hear something?"

A knocking had come from the hall door. "I shall see who it is," Lippo said.

He went out and crossed the sitting room to the suite's entrance. Hammond heard the door open, followed by a low-voiced inquiry. Then Lippo reappeared with a frightened look. He closed the office door and spoke in an undertone. "They wish to see you, *maestro*. One is a sheriff. The other shares a room with him."

Flint Hammond sat up rigidly, forcing himself to an appearance of composure. "You mean Harlan and Collier? Show them in, Lippo."

# Nine

Waiting, Hammond glanced uneasily toward a small steel safe. Was Sheriff Tucker sending them with a search warrant? Certain papers in that safe could destroy Hammond. Had Wesley Warren recovered his memory and told tales?

In a momentary panic Hammond took a gun from the desk drawer. He made sure it was loaded. Then, biting his lip, he put the gun out of sight again. Even if it were possible, shooting his way past them would do no good. Other officers would pick him up before he could leave town.

Again he filled his pipe, lighted it and sat puffing it in an effort to seem relaxed.

Two men came in and right away their lack of sternness reassured Hammond. Both were armed; yet both seemed not only friendly, but almost apologetic for intruding.

They stood hats in hand and Gerry Harlan, the giant deputy sheriff, had a grin on his wind-burned face. "Sorry to bust in on you like this, Mr. Hammond."

"It's my fault," insisted the cowboy known as John Collier. "I've been wanting to see you and tonight's the first chance I've had. So we stopped by for a minute on our way to bed."

"The desk clerk said you're still up," Harlan added.

The clerk would know that, Hammond thought, because he would have just seen Mel Janford come down the stairs after a call here. "Sit down, boys," Hammond invited. "What about a nightcap?"

"No thanks." Both callers remained standing. "Can't stay but a minute," Collier said. "Just want to thank you for offering to pay my hotel bill. But it won't be necessary. Tucker's put me on his payroll as a deputy and I can pay my own way. Thanks just the same."

To Hammond it seemed sincere and logical. A normal cowboy pride would incline Collier to react that way. It might embarrass him to have a stranger pay for his bed and board. So Flint Hammond didn't press the point. "I couldn't help wanting to do it," he explained. "Made me mad as hops, the idea of a pussyfooting waiter sneaking around the halls to dope coffeepots. Same thing might happen to me, or to one of my guests, any time. I often have people up here. Just wanted to help you nail that doper."

"He's nailed now," Gerry Harlan said grimly.

"Yes, so I heard. Tried to waylay you in a canyon, they say. That makes three times someone's tried to cash you in, eh, Collier?"

"Four," Collier corrected. He looked down at a bullet hole through his hat.

"Happened tonight right here on Harrison Avenue," Harlan said. "We were comin' home from supper at the Rands'."

"The devil you say! Got any idea who's back of it?"

"Not the foggiest," Collier said.

"We better not keep him up any longer, Johnnie," Harlan said. "You've had a long ride tonight, for a sick boy, and I'm putting you to bed. Good night, Mr. Hammond."

In a minute they were gone and the relief of it stood in moist beads on Hammond's forehead.

He made Lippo bring him another drink. "And bolt the hall door, Lippo."

Alone with his highball Hammond locked himself in the office. He went to his safe and took papers from it—two letters signed by Frank Bryson and a transfer of title signed by Job Norcross.

The letters could be burned but the title couldn't. The title wouldn't need to be re-recorded, however, unless or until Hammond should offer the *Morning Star* for sale. He had a receipt from the county clerk to prove that it had already been recorded once.

Now he looked closely at the syllable "Mor" which, if attention were called to it, would show that there'd been an erasure and a substitution. Inked writing could never be erased perfectly. A second erasure lower down suggested that a patent date had also been tampered with. Last January there'd been no reason for an over-worked copy clerk to give it close attention. There would be, however, if the paper was again left at Rand's office to be entered in a ledger.

That sharp-eyed daughter of Rand's had been alerted by Bryson's recent visit there.

What most concerned Hammond was the signa-ture of a Kansas City notary. The name, Walter Cummings, was clearly readable. But when copied into a ledger in the small cramped handwriting of Raymond Otis, who made a blunt top for an"m," an "n," an "i" or a "u," a reader might need a reading glass to make sure of the spelling.

Having made sure, Frank Bryson had written a letter addressed to Walter Cummings, Notary Public, Kansas City, Missouri. That letter had never been mailed. Flint Hammond now held it in his hand.

Also in his hand was a letter written and delivered to Wesley Warren, in care of the Bar F cattle ranch, Sidney, Nebraska. Both letters were on Clarendon Hotel stationery.

Before destroying them, Hammond reread them to make certain he'd overlooked nothing.

The one to the Nebraska cowboy said:

Dear Warren:

You'll recall that I met you in a bar at Sidney about two weeks ago. When I mentioned that I was on my way from Deadwood to Leadville, you told me you'd inherited from a Missouri uncle a half interest in a Leadville mine called the *Morning Star.* On his death bed the uncle told you the mine had never produced any silver and was probably worthless. But if I was going to Leadville anyway, would I be good enough to make sure? It might possibly have some small speculative value. I said I would. In the same conversation you mentioned that your uncle had also owned a half interest in a producing mine called the *Evening Star,* but that in order to pay medical bills he'd sold it to his partner.

When I got here I found that the *Evening Star* is now shut down; but that the *Morning Star* is a rich producer owned entirely by your uncle's ex-partner, Flint Hammond. I supposed that you'd simply gotten the names of the two mines mixed. To make sure I called on Mr. Hammond.

Hammond stopped reading to relight his pipe. He remembered his shock when the blunt Bryson, a man wise to the ways of mining camps, had approached him with an abrupt inquiry. And his own quick answer: "Yes, Mr. Bryson, it was his interest in the *Morning Star* that Job sold me. You'll find it on record at the county clerk's office. If you like, I can show you the letter Job wrote me offering to sell his share of the *Morning Star* for a thousand dollars."

He'd made a pretense of searching his desk for the letter. Then—"I remember now. It was brought to me while I was on a deerhunt at the head of Timberline Canyon, about three miles above the Breece Gulch store. First time I'm up there I'll bring it down. Or if you're in a hurry, you can ride up there yourself and have a look at it. The cabin's not locked. You'll find Job's letter in my leather hunting coat hanging on a wall peg."

Hammond continued reading:

I had no reason to doubt him. He'd hardly say that unless it was true. I spent the next day or two riding around looking for an investment of my own. Finally I found time to check on the *Morning Star* ownership at the county clerk's office. It was just as Hammond said; the property involved was the *Morning Star*, not the *Evening Star.* Then it occurred to me that by changing *"Eve"* to *"Mor"* Hammond could have switched the deal. I began to get vaguely suspicious and decided to have a look at your uncle's letter offering to sell. But before leaving the county clerk's office I made a note of the Missouri notary who'd notarized the transfer.

Then I rode to Timberline Canyon. A lonely place, eleven thousand feet above sea level. You don't hunt deer in January at that level; the snow would be ten feet deep. So I reconnoitered the cabin. When I peeked in at a window I didn't see any leather hunting coat on a wall peg. But I *did* see three riflemen waiting to crack down on someone. So it was a trap. Hammond had suckered me up there to be shot.

I got out of there fast and back to the hotel where I'm writing this letter. It might be that you're rich. Better come quick and find out. But you'll have to be careful. If you're being robbed, the man who's doing it lives right here at the Clarendon. It might be safer to register under another name until you've checked with me or consulted a good lawyer. Meantime I'll write that Kansas City notary and ask him for the name of the transferred property.

Yours truly,
*Frank Bryson*

The letter to the notary, taken unmailed from Bryson's body, had put a squeeze on Hammond and Janford. It warned them that Warren was on his way to Leadville. So beginning with the first stagecoach on which he could possibly arrive, they'd taken turn about watching for him. It was assumed he'd come to the Clarendon since Bryson had written him from there. As each coach from End-of-Track delivered passengers at the Clarendon, either Hammond or Janford was always buying a cigar at a nearby counter while newcomers registered. It was Janford who heard a young stranger with the look of a cowboy ask in what room he could find Frank Bryson.

"He's here, Flint," Janford had reported a few minutes later in Hammond's suite. "Using a phony name which shows he's got the wind up. Now that he knows Bryson's dead, chances are he'll go straight to a lawyer."

"We've got to head him off!" Hammond had muttered desperately.

"I'll see what I can do, Flint. I happen to know that a lawyer named Gentry is out of town today. Once we were on opposite sides of a court case and he called on me to propose a compromise. Left his card. Maybe I've still got it." Rummaging through his wallet Janford had taken out the professional card of one of his Leadville competitors. "Just sit tight, Flint, till you hear from me."

Not until later had Hammond learned how Janford had managed it. "I knocked at the cowboy's room and when he let me in, I handed him Lon Gentry's card. 'Mr. Frank Bryson,' I told him, 'made an appointment with me for last Saturday morning. He never kept it because Friday night he was murdered. I heard you ask about him at the desk just now. So maybe you know what he wanted to see me about.'

"He took a long hard look at the card and decided I was on the level. 'It's a long story, Mr. Gentry,' he said. 'Come in and let's talk it over.'

"I looked at my watch. 'I've a client waiting for me right now. Be through with him in an hour. Why don't you come to my office an hour from now. It's up on Poplar Street. Anyone can point it out to you.'

" 'Okay, Mr. Gentry,' he said. With that I breezed on down the hall and got busy setting up the deadfall. It was that easy, Flint."

Now Flint Hammond struck a match and burned both letters. He put the title itself back in his safe. Then he unlocked the office door and called in Lippo.

"We were talking about your wife, Lippo."

"Yes," the Italian prompted eagerly. "You will send for her?"

Hammond answered indirectly. "Write her to ride a D & R G train to Canon City and there catch a stagecoach for Leadville. Only she's not to come all the way. She must get off the stage at Buena Vista."

Lippo gave a puzzled stare. Buena Vista was thirty-five miles southeast of Leadville, where the Canon City stage road crossed Cottonwood Creek.

"Now listen carefully, Lippo. Eight miles up Cottonwood Creek from Buena Vista, in a fir forest, there's a log hunting lodge built last spring by a New York millionaire. He furnished it completely, spared no expense to make it comfortable, planning to take eastern friends there for hunting and fishing during summer months. Then he died of a heart attack before he had a chance to use it."

Hammond took another drink, while Lippo waited in confusion.

"His widow," Hammond resumed, "has no use for the place. Immediately she offered to sell or lease it. Through an agent I leased it for one year. The name I leased it under is Clemson. Here is the key, Lippo."

As he accepted the key, Lippo began to understand. Himself a fugitive from Italian justice, he could appreciate the value and convenience of a pre-prepared hideaway.

"I can never tell when I might need it, Lippo. If and when I do, it will be sudden. I'd need to ride fast and secretly to that lodge in the woods.

And I like my comforts, Lippo. If I should arrive in the middle of a dark, cold night I want to find a blazing hearth waiting for me. With plenty of food and wine, and with you and Marta to look after me. Do you understand?"

"You have made it clear, *signor.*"

"Very well. When Marta gets off the stage at Buena Vista, you will meet her with a buckboard. The buckboard will be loaded with food and wine—whatever is needed for your comfort and mine. I may never join you. Let's hope I won't have to. But if I do . . ."

"All will be ready," promised Lippo.

# Ten

The roaring, gaudy life of Leadville boomed on, through night shifts and day shifts, its people carting ore from hundreds of shafts on Fryer and Carbonate and Breece Hills to the smoky smelters of California Gulch. Twenty thousand lusty miners continued to dig by day and revel by night, or vice versa, swarming from the shafts at each shift's end to the bars and games of a camp both fabulously rich and shamelessly corrupt—where an endless chain of stagecoaches brought in an overflow which often had to sleep in the streets.

Saloonmen and speculators alike were pulling

in money hand over fist. Each week a long queue of lewd women lined up to pay fines at the city hall, from there parading brazenly back to their trade. Bunco men thrived on the street corners, fleecing victims in broad daylight, always knowing just which lawmen could be counted on to look the other way. Five variety theaters peddled cham-pagne and burlesque from noon till dawn, while seventeen smelters turned out a ton of solid silver a day and the killings averaged one a night. The city's two jails were full, their small, filthy iron cages crammed with pickpockets and murderers all scheming to get out by bail or bribe, with neither Tucker nor Duggan ever quite sure which turnkeys they could trust.

The hundred bars were full of talk—much of it about the mystery of John Collier and the four attempts on his life. And since a good deal of it was guess talk, gradually it focused on the two known devils in the brew, Culp and Murdy.

Culp they couldn't get at. He was still at large and smart enough to stay that way. But Murdy was caged. He could be had, the bar crowds said.

A man at the Odeon stared blearily into his beer. "He'd orter be strung up by the thumbs till he tells who the heck's backin' him."

"By the thumbs or by the neck," another agreed.

The bartender offered a word. "There's big money in the deal, somewhere. The Culp gang don't hire out fer chicken feed. What with stealin' ledgers and drygulching deputies, somebody must be puttin' up real dough."

"The way I heard it, Ace, them deputies fetched back a hot clew from that Timberline cabin. It was locked in a drawer at Tucker's office—but come mornin' it was gone."

"Did they fire the property clerk?"

"Nope. They can't prove nothin' on him. Lots of crooked clerks and deputies have been fired in the last year and any one of 'em could have taken an office key with him. That Culp gang always did have a pipeline right into the courthouse and city hall."

"They need sweepin' out, both them places, Luke."

"What's needed most," Luke insisted, "is a rope around Murdy's neck. Hoist him a coupla feet off the ground and he'll tell who the payoff man is."

The same talk was going on along the walks. John Collier and Gerry Harlan heard snatches of it on their way down Harrison to the sheriff's office.

Tucker himself had heard it and was more than worried. Twice already this year a prisoner had been snatched by a mob and lynched.

"There's just one way to make sure," Tucker said as he lighted another stogie, "that it don't happen to Murdy."

"What's that?" Collier asked him.

The office was milling with deputies, clerks, lawyers and visitors entering and leaving the cell block, as well as citizens paying fees or making complaints. For privacy Tucker led the way into his own cubbyhole and closed the door. "I don't want this to leak out, boys. But I'm shipping Murdy over to Fair Play. Fair Play's got a good stout jail and there's no feeling against Murdy in that county. It oughta keep him safe till trial day."

"You'll send him over on a stage?" Harlan asked.

"No. A stagecoach is too public. I'll send him over horseback by night, with three deputies guarding him."

"Which three?" Collier asked.

"You and Gerry for two. I'll let Tom Trevor side you. Tom used to be a stage driver on the Mosquito Pass run and he can follow that trail on the darkest night. You oughta make Alma for breakfast and ride into Fair Play by noon."

"Suits me," Collier said. He touched a bullet hole through the crown of his hat and added with a grin, "It beats staying cooped in a hotel room waiting to be sneaked up on."

"It's a smart idea, Sheriff," Gerry Harlan said. "There's plenty of rope talk around town. They'd a heap rather have Harry the fake waiter—the one who slipped a shot of dope to Cal Barstow. But Harry's in the morgue along with Gil Hocker. Only one they can lay hands on is Murdy."

Tucker puffed smoke from his stogie, then lowered his voice. "It's not only a lynch mob we have to watch out for. Murdy's own crowd wouldn't mind snuffing him out either. Long as he's alive he can talk. Some big money man's back of all this and he's sitting on two sharp needles. One of 'em's you, Collier, who might get your memory back any minute. The other's Murdy, who might talk to save his neck."

That angle hadn't occurred to Collier. He listened to footsteps and a jangle of voices from the main office—officers, visitors, lawyers, bail-bond men. Among them might be an assassin with the assignment of stopping Murdy's mouth.

Gerry asked, "Does Murdy know he's taking a ride tonight?"

"Nobody knows except the three of us and Trevor. We won't tell Murdy till we boost him into a saddle."

There was a knock and Deputy Steve Loftus came in. "Telegram from California, Sheriff."

It was from California's attorney general.

"I asked him about Rails, Yeager and Chandler," Tucker said after reading it. "He says no one by those names is wanted in California. Which proves nothing. A wanted killer would be using a different name now."

"What about the gink named Joe?" Gerry asked.

"We can't pick him up," Tucker admitted. "We don't know which Joe he is. Duggan figures he's a ringer spotted to plant a phony rumor and make us look for the wrong man."

Loftus returned to his routine duties and Tucker gave final instructions to Harlan and Collier. "I want you boys to sleep all afternoon because you'll be riding all night. Report here right after dark and Trevor'll have the horses ready. And keep a close mouth about it."

At noon Collier and Harlan crossed to the county clerk's office where Angela Rand had been helping out all morning. "You'd better not let her old man see you takin' her out," Gerry said. "He expects you to be shot at any minute." Angela had promised Collier to go to lunch with him at the Clarendon.

A queue of property owners stood in line with titles they wanted to leave for re-recording. The bad news about the burning of Book B was leaking out. "There'll be a line a block long," Milton Rand grumbled, "when everybody finds out about it." He'd already hired an extra copy clerk to help Raymond Otis.

Angela put on her hat and came out into the entry where Gerry Harlan, looming at Collier's elbow, made a grimace of apology. "Three's a crowd, Angela. But don't blame *me*. I've got orders not to let this bullet bait get ten feet away from me, day or night."

"Please see that you don't," Angela said quickly. "But that needn't bother us. Why don't we take a cab and pick up Lola?"

"You just read my mind," Gerry said. He went out and whistled for a hack.

Presently the hack delivered them and Lola Loomis to the Clarendon. The usual noon crowd was there. They'd have to wait their turn for a table, a waiter said. He led them to a divan just inside the dining room. It was meant for three people but the four of them managed to squeeze into it. "Johnnie and I don't mind," Gerry grinned.

Angela began pointing out celebrities to Collier. "There's Mr. August Meyer eating with Governor Tabor. That couple in the corner is Mayor James and his wife. Vic Werner of the *Little Eva* is joining them now."

"Don't overlook Flint Hammond," Gerry put in. "The two guys with him are Fryer and Berdell. More millionaires around here than you could shake a stick at. And dogged if there isn't that little Dutch shoemaker, Rische. Wonder what he'll do with the three hundred thousand Tabor bought him out for."

"Isn't that our friend the reporter?"

The others followed Collier's gaze toward Barry Holden who was moving briskly about with an open notebook, stopping at first one table and then at another.

"Busy bird-dogging a story, I suppose," Lola murmured.

"Most of the big fellows eat here," Harlan said, "so it's a good place for Barry to get wind of any new deal on the fire. He'll be headin' this way, Johnnie, soon as he spots you. He'll want to know how many times you've been sniped at since breakfast."

It drew a reproachful look from Angela. "Don't let Dad hear you talk like that, Gerry. He already thinks I keep dangerous company. So he's trying to ship me off to Aunt Minnie in Denver."

"Maybe he's right," John Collier said soberly.

"Nonsense!" To shift the subject Angela resumed pointing out notables. "The one Barry's talking to right now is Tom Walsh. He used to run the Grand Hotel but now he owns the *Camp Bird* mine and is a millionaire."

"Almost everybody is," Gerry complained, "except me and Johnnie."

They saw Barry Holden move on to a table where a sleek, muscular man with a ruddy face and roached hair was eating alone. "That's Melville Janford," Angela said.

From her tone Collier sensed that she didn't like Janford. "What's the matter with him?" he asked.

"Nothing, I suppose. Except that he's always snooping around the county offices and I suspect he's looking for scandals. Dad says he's a good title lawyer; but I can't quite trust him."

Holden was standing by Janford's table with a bantering smile, asking what seemed to be casual questions. But the lawyer didn't appreciate them. At first he seemed only mildly annoyed.

In a moment some question from the reporter made the lawyer stand up with an angry rush of blood to his cheeks.

The four waiting on the divan gazed curiously that way. Standing, Janford loomed a head taller than the bantam reporter. They saw Barry ask one more question and this time the answer was a punch to the chin.

Barry Holden went down and out, the lawyer towering red-tempered over him. On all sides there were exclamations of surprise and dismay from waiters and other diners. The first to reach the stunned newsman was Flint Hammond. The next was the hotel's proprietor, Mr. Bush. From the circle around Barry Holden came voices: "He's out cold! A cut chin and a lump where his head hit the floor." Then Flint Hammond's voice: "Better take him up to my suite, Mr. Bush. Lippo can give him first aid till Doc Fowler comes."

"Thank you, Mr. Hammond." The hotel man called a pair of waiters. The lawyer Janford hadn't reseated himself. Stares at him from the other diners weren't friendly.

Angela whispered, "Barry's popular and *he* isn't."

Then Collier heard Janford's voice, half truculent and half apologetic. "Sorry, Mr. Bush. I just don't like being insulted."

No one asked him the nature of Holden's insult. Two waiters picked up the unconscious reporter and carried him out. People began reseating themselves. One of those still standing was Flint Hammond and he spoke in a tone of sharp reproof. "You didn't have to get so rough with him, Janford."

Vic Werner called from across the room. "Why can't you pick on someone your size?"

The lawyer snapped back: "*Your* size will do, any time you feel like it. I'll be in the bar if anyone wants to make something of it." He walked stiffly out of the dining room.

"He's not usually like that," Angela said. "Barry must have hit a nerve, somewhere. I wonder what about."

A table was now ready and a waiter led them to it. As they gave their orders Collier looked out into the lobby and saw Doctor Fowler. Satchel in hand, the doctor was on his way up to Hammond's suite to attend Holden.

They'd almost finished eating when Fowler came down again.

Angela wrote a note on her menu and handed it to a waiter, who took it across the room to Flint Hammond. After reading it, Hammond smiled at Angela and gave a nod.

"I asked," she explained, "if we might go up to see Barry."

Presently they arrived at a second-floor door over which hung a silver horseshoe. Lippo opened it and let them into a sitting room where Barry Holden lay on a couch with a pillow back of his head. He was in good spirits. "Hi, neighbors! How did you like the brawl? I walked right into it, didn't I?"

"What on earth," Angela demanded, "did you say to him?"

The reporter grinned. "Pull up a chair, folks, and I'll let you in on it."

Lippo came in noiselessly with a tray. The tray had four glasses of sherry. Each of the visitors accepted one and sat down.

"I was out last night with Oscar Ashley," Barry confided. "Oscar's a teller at the Raynolds bank. A teller's not supposed to talk about a customer's account but after three beers Oscar's tongue loosened a little."

"About Janford's account?" Harlan prompted.

Barry nodded. "There was nothing wrong with it. Oscar just said that every Monday morning for the last eight weeks Janford has made a cash deposit of about seven hundred dollars. 'So what?' I said. Sometimes a lawyer takes a case on a contingent fee basis. Nothing if he loses; and if he wins a certain per cent of the client's gain. I figured Mel Janford must have hit a jackpot like that. Maybe some mine had gone into bonanza and as its lawyer Janford was pulling in so much a week. That's the way I doped it and so did Oscar Ashley."

"But it was something else?"

"I forgot all about it," Barry said, "till I happened to see Janford in the dining room today. 'When are you going to retire, Mel?' I asked, just to kid him a little. Right away he got cagey. 'What do you mean?' he came back. So I said, 'With seven hundred a week you'll be retiring pretty soon, won't you? Who've you got the goods on, Mel?' "

"He thought you really meant it?"

"He sure did. And the shoe must've fit pretty tight because he got scared, then mad, then madder. So I kept baiting him to see what kind of a rise I could get."

"What was your payoff question?" Collier asked.

"It was a shot in the dark," the reporter admitted. "I asked him, 'It wouldn't have anything to do with the Bryson case, would it?' Right then he socked me."

# Eleven

As darkness deepened over Leadville Collier and Harlan walked down Harrison to the county jail. At least a hundred muttering men were milling about at the corner of Elm and Harrison.

"And more coming, Johnnie. Getting Murdy through them might not be easy."

To avoid the crowd the two deputies circled to an alley and entered the jail by its back door. Passing up an aisle between cages they saw Murdy with a pasty fear on his face. Street sounds had reached him and he knew what they were. "You dassent let 'em take me!" he whined.

"We won't if we can help it," Harlan promised. He moved on a step or two, then turned back. "That neck of yours isn't hardly worth saving, Murdy. But we might try a little harder if you'd tip us off who's backing you."

Murdy's prepared answer came in a husky whisper. "Sure I will. His name's Donlavey and he hangs out at the American Hotel."

Harlan eyed him skeptically. "Donlavey? Never heard of him."

"He ain't the top man," Murdy confided. "He's only a go-between. Donlavey never told me who he reports to. Might be Haw Tabor himself, fer all I know."

"Sol Lenniger," Collier reminded him, "was the name you conjured up when I caught you sawing through my door."

In the front office they joined Sheriff Tucker. "Ever hear of anyone named Donlavey, Sheriff?"

Tucker smiled cryptically. "So he gave you that name too! He's just handing it out to fool us, boys. I checked at the American. Their book shows that a Donlavey was there two weeks ago and stayed four days. Where he went nobody knows. I'll lay odds he's got nothing to do with Bryson. Or with you either, Collier."

Harlan was equally sure of it. "A guy rich enough to foot the bill for what's goin' on wouldn't stay at a third-rate joint like the American." He went to a front window, looked out and saw that the street crowd had doubled.

A little way down Elm a man standing on a beer keg was making a speech. What he said brought a rumble of assent from the crowd and there was a coiled rope in his hands.

"They're a pack of likkered-up bar bums," Gerry said. "I'd hate to shoot one of 'em, just to protect a skunk like Murdy."

"You won't have to," Tucker said. "Tom Trevor's a block east of here with the horses. And I just sent Dad Hixon to circulate through the crowd. Hixon," he explained to Collier, "is an undercover come-on man we use sometimes. He looks and talks like a hoodlum."

"What's his play?" Gerry asked.

"He's plantin' a phony tip. It's to make 'em believe we moved Murdy down to the city jail this afternoon."

Duggan's jail was at the foot of Pine, a long block west of here and in the opposite direction from where Trevor was waiting with horses.

A grim smile rode Tucker's plump face as he looked from a front window. The crowd was already drifting down Elm toward Pine. "Duggan won't like it when they bust in on him. But they'll leave just as soon as they find out Murdy's not there. Get ready to ride, boys."

Harlan took two rifles from the riot rack, handed one of them to Collier. "Let's get started, Johnnie."

A minute later they were leading Murdy from his cage. Tucker made the man slip on a high-collared sheepskin coat, then put handcuffs on him. "Take him out the back way, boys."

The alley was dark and quiet. From it the deputies hustled Murdy east across a vacant lot to Plum Street and found Tom Trevor waiting there. He had four strong horses each with a slicker and a mackinaw back of its saddle. "It'll be cold as Pharaoh's heart up on Mosquito Pass," he predicted.

They boosted Murdy to a saddle.

The prisoner rattled his handcuffs, mumbling, "Have I got to ride with these on?"

"You bet," Trevor said, "and with a stirrup iron too." He snapped a second manacle on Murdy's left ankle, linking it to the stirrup. "Just to make sure you don't slip away in the dark."

The three deputies mounted and Trevor, a chunky ex–stage driver, led the way easterly to Oak, then up Oak to Jefferson. The stage road to Fair Play ran out Jefferson and they moved along it at a trot.

"We got to make time while we can," Trevor

said. "After we pass Yankee Hill the grade'll hold us to a walk, all the way to the pass."

"How far is it?" Collier asked.

"Thirty-five miles to Fair Play but only thirteen miles to Mosquito Pass. Rubs the sky, that pass does. Stage line only uses it in summer. Five months of the year it's snowed in. In winter the coaches have to take the longer route over Weston Pass, south of here."

On the hillsides lamps and torches flickered from a hundred mines. Loaded carts passed them, since most of the big producers ran night and day. The road itself was dark and cartmen weren't likely to recognize Murdy. To lessen the chance of it Trevor pulled the prisoner's hat over his eyes. "We don't want 'em to tip off that lynch mob till we get you over the pass."

They veered to the right up Little Strayhorse Gulch on a route which took them between Fryer and Yankee Hills. After an hour of steady, silent riding the mine lights began thinning out. A stagecoach met them, its six horses moving at a downhill trot. "A McClellan and Spottswood outfit," Harlan told Collier. "They run four coaches a day each way between Leadville and End-of-Track."

"They tell me I came in on a Barlow and Sanderson coach," Collier said. "But you can't prove it by me."

"Four stage lines altogether," Trevor said. "The

one from Georgetown's the roughest. But this one's the highest." He pointed to the outline of a snowy peak limned against the stars. "That's Mount Evans. We cross just to the left of it."

Eight miles and two hours out of Leadville the trail took an abrupt turn to the north. An icy wind blew down from Mount Evans and the deputies put on their mackinaws. Here they were beyond the mine lights and presently they were riding through a mountain park where slim, white-barked aspens hemmed them on either side.

"You oughta thank us, Murdy," Trevor said, "fer savin' yer ornery neck. If you had a spark of gratitude you'd tell us who paid you the five thousand dollars fer sawin' through Johnnie's door."

"I already told you," the prisoner muttered sullenly. "His name's Donlavey."

"Trouble is we don't believe you," Trevor argued. "Tell us somethin' we can check on—like where's Gus Culp's hide-out. Gus must have at least ten cutthroats sidin' him; and they've got to eat and sleep somewhere."

"Is it some dive in Leadville?" Harlan prodded. "Or some hideaway in the hills?"

"How would I know?" Murdy whined.

"Then who was it sent you and Hocker and Tipper Harry out to drygulch me and Johnnie Collier? Don't tell us it was someone named

Donlavey or Lenniger. You can't fake-name your way out of this, Murdy."

No answer from Murdy. Presently a light showed beside the trail ahead, close-hemmed by the aspen forest. In a minute Collier made out the shapes of buildings and corrals. "The Mosquito Park relay station," Trevor said. "Shall we ask for fresh horses, Gerry?"

After weighing the idea Harlan turned it down. The relay station had a bar and someone there might spread the news about shifting Murdy over the pass. "I'm not worryin' about the lynch mob, Tom. Those bums wouldn't fork a saddle this far even to hang Murdy. It's Culp and his outfit we'd better watch out for."

"We'd be set-ups," Trevor agreed, "if they were waitin' for us in the pass. Two shots from the dark would take care of both Collier and Murdy."

"Why *me?*" Murdy protested.

"To shut your mouth," Harlan said. "You haven't named Mr. Big yet. But how do they know you won't?"

Murdy shivered and didn't answer. For a minute the only sounds were hoof thuds. Then Gerry Harlan spoke again, thinking aloud. "We've had leaks at the county offices. Take that property clerk who let a specs case disappear from a locked drawer. Chances are he was bribed. For another bribe he might've tipped 'em off about our switchin' Murdy to Fair Play."

They rode silently past the Mosquito Park station and continued on upmountain. The trees ended abruptly, with nothing beyond them except rock and snow. "We're about eleven and a half thousand feet high here," Trevor said. "The pass is a little over twelve."

"In two or three places," Gerry told Collier, "the timberline dips almost down to Leadville."

From here the trail was a zigzag staircase of switchbacks with snow patches gleaming under the stars. The horses were blowing hard as they made the last steep summit climb to a niche between gaunt crags.

"Straight up midnight," Trevor said after looking at his watch.

Collier felt the chill of altitude biting him. "No wonder they don't use this pass in wintertime!"

"We drop down fast from here," Trevor said. "The London Hill relay station's only four mile below here. We can warm up with coffee and get fresh horses."

"That oughta hold us," Harlan said, "till we get breakfast at Alma."

Collier asked, "Do these relay stations stay open all night?"

"They have to, with a coach due every six hours both ways. Lots of times they run late, so the stations have to be ready."

"Ready with grub and liquor," Tom Trevor added. "You'd be surprised how much grub and liquor a coachful of passengers can lap up."

They rode on down the east slope and in half an hour came to timberline again. Last winter's snow still made patches of white on either side. The first trees were scrub aspen which soon merged with spruce and fir. Far down the range they heard the bugle of an elk.

"Feel better now?" Harlan asked the prisoner. "By noon you'll be in jail at Fair Play where nobody's got it in for you. Your neck'll be safe till court day."

Again Collier saw the lights of a relay station and a little after one they drew up there. After dismounting, Trevor released a stirrup link from Murdy's ankle.

A hostler came out with a lantern. "We're from the Lake County sheriff's office," Harlan said. "What about four fresh saddle mounts?"

"Right this way." The hostler moved toward a stable.

"I'll take Murdy inside," Trevor said, "and have 'em heat up some coffee."

He led the prisoner into the station while Collier and Harlan followed the hostler to the barn.

The hostler's lantern played eerily along the barn aisle and Collier saw four horses waiting. An odd thing was that the mounts were already saddled.

"How did you know we were coming?" he asked.

"Them other two deputies," the station man

explained, "told us you'd get here about one o'clock. They said to have fresh horses ready so you could push right along."

Harlan stood gaping. "What other two deputies?"

"Them two what rode ahead of you to make sure you wouldn't run into no trouble. They—"

"What did they look like?"

"They had badges on. Big guy and a little guy. Big guy had a spade beard and walked with a limp."

Gerry Harlan whipped around toward Collier. "Sounds like Gus Culp, Johnnie."

"So does *that!*" Collier said. He rushed from the stable and headed for the station's eating house. Two rifle shots had just jarred the darkness in that direction.

Harlan, gun out, kept pace with him. From beyond the station came the hoofbeats of retreating horsemen. "Two of 'em, sounds like," Gerry said. "Two snipers and two shots—one meant for you and one for Murdy."

They reached the station and burst into a long public room which had a bar at one end and tables at another. On the woods side of it was a smashed window where Trevor and a night cook stood staring helplessly out into darkness. In timber beyond the window the hoof sounds of two horsemen faded out.

"Caught me flat-footed," Trevor said bitterly.

"You can't hardly foller 'em in the dark," the

night cook said. "Looks like it's a clean getaway."

Harlan looked grimly at John Collier. "Lucky you went to the barn with me, Johnnie. If you'd come in here with Murdy they'd 've nailed both of you."

Collier, looking down at a handcuffed man on the floor, could hardly doubt it. Murdy had two body bullets and was dead.

# Twelve

The three impatient deputies stood in an aspen copse back of the London Hill station. "We're stymied till daybreak," Harlan fretted. They were waiting with fresh horses, ready to track the outlaws who'd shot Murdy.

"Right here's where their sign begins," Trevor said, "but we'll need bright light to follow it."

Collier looked at two 44-40 empties in the palm of his hand—used rifle shells he'd picked up under the station window. From there, using a lantern, they'd followed the footprints of two men a hundred yards to a spot in the trees where two mounts had been tethered. "Looks like they took off due south," Harlan said. "Culp and one of his heelers. My guess is they'll head back to their Leadville hide-out."

With exasperating slowness the light brightened. At five o'clock the station man came out with a food pack. Trevor tied it back of his cantle. "They'll lead us a long chase," he reckoned.

"The next westbound stage makes a breakfast stop here," the station man said. "I'll send word to Sheriff Tucker by the driver."

"You can hold Murdy's body for the coroner," Harlan said. "Let's hit the saddle, boys."

The three deputies mounted and rode single file through the trees. Trevor, in the lead, could dimly make out the hoofprints of the retreating outlaws. At this altitude nearly every afternoon brought a shower of rain. It made a soft bed for hoof marks except where there was an outcropping of rock. "Ten to one they won't risk trailing back over Mosquito Pass," Trevor said.

Harlan was equally sure of it. "Next gap south of here's Weston Pass. It'd take 'em to Leadville by a long roundabout route. Or they could take off down Sacramento Gulch to Fair Play."

"My money says they'll head for Leadville," Trevor argued. "They haven't got any deals at Fair Play but they've got plenty at Leadville."

The fugitive sign came to a game trail and followed it southerly along a wooded sidehill slope. Mount Evans loomed to the west with fingers of snow reaching down its crevices toward them. Twice the tracks crossed hard-caked snowdrifts, leaving deep, shod prints. Once the outlaws had veered well downslope to detour a drift too deep for the horses.

"Here's the head of Sacramento Gulch," Trevor announced presently, "and they didn't turn down it."

Which indicated that Culp and his men weren't going to Fair Play or End-of-Track, or anywhere else in the vast basin of South Park lying directly east of this range. "Why should they," Gerry reasoned, "when they've got big money on tap at Leadville?"

"They're four hours ahead of us," Trevor calculated. "So they could beat us to Leadville and get lost there."

"My hunch is," Gerry countered, "that they'll head for some woods hideaway. If we can trail 'em there we can shoot it out. What say, Johnnie?"

"Suits me," Collier said.

Late morning brought them to the head of Horseshoe Gulch in a smooth aspen park just below timberline. A cow elk browsing there with her calf went trotting off through the trees. Horseshoe Peak, looming fourteen thousand feet high, touched the clouds only two eagle-flight miles west of them. The fugitive sign was skirting timberline and keeping roughly parallel to the backbone of the range. Twice in the next hour Trevor lost the tracks on rocky balds. Each time they reappeared just inside the tree line.

"They're headed for Weston Pass," Harlan concluded.

Trevor pointed to a circle of silvery water a

short way down the slope. "That's Twelve Mile Lake. Lays between two forks of Twelve Mile Creek straight upmountain from Fair Play." He twisted in his saddle to point in the opposite direction. "And that's Ptarmagan Peak right above us. Weston Pass is a gap on the south shoulder of Ptarmagan."

They halted where snow water made a trickle across the trail. Cured bluestem grew in a swale there and Trevor let the mounts graze for half an hour. Harlan unwrapped the food pack and Collier made a fire. Even in August the air had a glacial chill.

"Suppose we track 'em to a hide-out," Trevor said. "What then?"

"We might need help," Gerry admitted, "to outgun those birds. Culp could have seven or eight men at his hideaway. The way I figure it, that's too many to keep a secret. Murdy didn't talk; but they were afraid he would. If we can gun down a few of those birds and toss the rest in jail, one of 'em oughta crack and tell us who the payoff man is."

"Which is the one we want," Trevor agreed. "The guy Bryson had the goods on." He looked sideways at John Collier. "Likely *you've* got the deadwood on him too, Johnnie. Only you just can't recollect what it is."

"If Mr. Big can manage it," Gerry put in grimly, "Johnnie won't live to remember. That fella's spendin' money like a drunken sailor. Five thousand at one crack to Murdy. What he's paid out to Culp and Hocker and the rest we'll never know."

Trevor gathered up the horses. "We're burning daylight, pardners."

They pushed on and in less than an hour came to a deep-rutted road twisting upward toward Weston Pass. Freighting outfits had moved along it today, making ox tracks, wheel tracks, horse tracks both shod and unshod.

The Culp sign didn't cross the road to continue into timber beyond. So the outlaws had either turned downtrail into South Park or uptrail toward Weston Pass.

Without even discussing it the deputies turned uptrail. Only by going that way could Gus Culp return to his Leadville operations.

At the summit they found an eastbound wagoneer resting his mules. Harlan questioned him. "Two guys must've passed you on jaded horses. They carry rifles and holster guns. One of 'em's got a beard. Remember seein' 'em?"

"Not in the last few hours," the wagoneer said.

The deputies rode on and a mile down the slope met another freighter. The same question drew the same answer.

"It don't mean a thing," Tom Trevor concluded as they rode on. "When Culp sees a wagon coming he can draw off in the woods a piece till it passes. As a long-time outlaw he'd have lots of practice doing that."

Ahead of them the sun dipped behind the snowy summits of the Sawatch divide and the cool of twilight came on. At the next bend they found a stage station used only in winter when the Spottswood coaches from Fair Play took this longer route. Now the place had only a stock tender.

"If them outlaws passed here," he told Gerry Harlan, "I never seen 'em. But I was off grouse huntin' half the afternoon."

There was an hour of twilight left when the deputies rode on. Light lasted till they came to Zeke Olney's trailside store at Empire Creek. They questioned Olney. "If them guys came along here," the storeman said, "they detoured me. I got a stew on the stove, boys. Help yourself. And they's some bunks in the back room if you wanta stay all night."

Fagged and famished, the deputies accepted promptly. "Looks like we've been ridin' the skin off our saddles all for nothing," Trevor said. "By morning the trail'll be too old and cold. Even if we see horse tracks turning off the road we won't know who made 'em."

"And if they stay *on* the road," Harlan said, "the dust of some Leadville back street'll swallow 'em."

They helped themselves to venison stew. Then

an idle question from John Collier led to a new straw of hope. "How's business?" Collier asked the storeman.

"It ain't been worth shucks," Zeke Olney complained, "since the Mallory mine shut down. It went into litigation about two months ago, and each side got a court injunction to stop the other side from operating. Used to be forty men workin' there and I sold 'em a lot of likker and groceries. Now there's nobody but a caretaker."

"The Mallory's up Iowa Gulch, ain't it?" Trevor prompted. "Last winter I usta drop off mail for 'em at the gulch crossing, when I drove a Spottswood stage on the Weston Pass route."

"That's right," Olney said. "The mine buildings are about two mile upgulch from the stage road. Drinks a heap o' likker, that caretaker does. I been sellin' him a case a week. Don't see how one man can soak up that much."

"Neither do I," Collier agreed thoughtfully. "Maybe he's not alone up there. What does he look like?"

"Skinny red-neck with a hard, bony face," the storeman said. "Wears a forty-four gun with a bone grip. . . . What's the matter?"

A startled look on Collier's face matched the one on Harlan's. "Sounds like Gil Hocker!" Gerry exclaimed. "But Hocker's been dead four days."

"It's been a week since I've seen him," the storeman said.

Harlan turned with a jerk to Trevor. "Looks like we've hit pay dirt, Tom. What better hideaway could they want than a shut-down mine up a lonely gulch? Handy, too. Not over six miles from Leadville."

"They were headin' right toward it," Trevor agreed. "Culp and his London Hill sniper."

"A case of whisky a week!" Harlan brooded. "Take at least seven men to swill down that much, and stay sober enough to cut throats. We'll saddle up at daybreak and tie into 'em."

The back room cots were hard and the blankets thin. Collier got up stiff and shivering when Olney wakened them at dawn. "Can't see what yer hurry is," the storeman said as he served them a sowbelly breakfast. "Them hideout fellers'll keep. After a fast sweat-ride from London Hill yesterday they'll likely sleep all day."

The horses had been grained overnight and were ready for travel. By seven o'clock the three deputies were spurring down the stage road. A mile and a half brought them to Iowa Gulch which had a small flow of snow water. A wooden sign there had two pointing fingers. The one pointing down the stage road said, "Leadville, 4 miles." The one pointing upgulch said, "Mallory mine, 2 miles."

"Right here's where I dropped off their mail last winter," Trevor said. He dismounted for a close look at the gravel. "Can't be sure; but I'd say two horsemen turned up this gulch since the last shower."

They rode cautiously upgulch, staying off the ore cart trail which led up the east side and keeping to the west side where the pine timber grew thickest. "Peel your eyes for a lookout," Trevor advised. "If they's a nest of outlaws at that mine they might post a sentry. Don't let him see us first."

In half an hour they sighted the mine. There were two shaft houses, an administration building, a superintendent's residence, a long bunkhouse, a stable, a blacksmith shop and tool sheds. Only the superintendent's house showed smoke at its chimney. No guard had been posted.

A wagon yard had carts in it and a corral contained what looked like a dray team. No saddle horses were in sight. Trevor scouted ahead to peer through an opening in the trees. In a moment he signaled Collier and Harlan to join him. "We better check the stable and count saddles."

"Right, Tom," Gerry agreed. "No use starting a fight till we know what we're up against."

They tied their mounts in a pinery and moved forward afoot with rifles. Across the gulch they could see the cart road on which ore had been hauled to the Leadville smelters. The entire mining claim, three hundred feet wide by fifteen hundred long, had a high wire fence around it with a padlocked gate at the cart road.

When they were opposite the gate Trevor stopped them. "You boys watch the road and the super's house, in case anyone comes out. I'll circle to the back of the stable and count broncs."

He disappeared into the trees, following the claim's westerly fence. Collier and Harlan kept out of sight and quiet, watching the gate and the front of the house. In a little while they saw a man come out with a water bucket. He was a short man in a buckskin coat and denim pants, bareheaded. The tip of a holster showed below the edge of his coat.

The watchers saw him fill the bucket at a well and go back inside. Another ten minutes went by with no sign of life except smoke rising from the house chimney.

Then the same man came out again and this time he went to the stable. Gerry Harlan whispered, "He'll be feeding whatever stock's in there."

If the man ran into Tom Trevor there'd be shooting. In which case others in the house would rush out to help the choreman. "Get ready to pick 'em off, Johnnie." Harlan poked his rifle through the fence wires to cover a path between house and barn.

Collier did the same, but there was no need to shoot. The choreman drove the two dray horses from the corral into the stable. Presently he went back to the house, relaxed and whistling.

Then Trevor reappeared, slipping like an Indian through the pines. "I tore my britches," he said wryly, "climbin' that danged fence. Seven saddles in the barn; and nine horses if you count a wagon team. A guy showed up to feed 'em but he didn't see me."

"Recognize him?"

"I sure did. He's a bad actor named Buckshot Joe Wofford. Him and a couple of guys held up my stage one time between Alma and Mosquito Pass."

"What else did you see in there?"

"I felt of the seven saddle blankets. Two of 'em are still a little damp from a hard ride a couple of 'em made yesterday from London Hill. Other five are bone dry." Tom Trevor cocked an eye as he licked a cigaret. "What do you say, pardners? Shall we whang into 'em?"

As the senior deputy Gerry Harlan weighed it carefully, torn between two pulls. One impulse was to shoot it out, here and now, and damn the odds. In the end the other pull decided him.

"It's like this, Tom. Tucker gave me the assignment of keeping Johnnie alive. Steering him into a three-against-seven gunfight ain't the best way to do it. Maybe we could down most of 'em, but there'd be hits on both sides. One of 'em could be Johnnie Collier."

"Forget it!" Collier broke in impatiently. "I'd be

141

taking the same chance you are. I say let's tie into 'em right now."

Harlan shook his head. "Wouldn't matter much if Tom or me took a bullet or two. But there's big doings riding on your life, Johnnie. You're the key to the whole mess, Tucker claims. If they gun you down you'll never live to tell us why the heck you came to Leadville."

Trevor started to light his cigaret, then dropped the match and stepped on it. "Gerry's right, Johnnie. We'd better even up the odds a little before we start throwing lead."

Gerry produced a coin. "We'll flip for it, Tom. My orders are to stick with Johnnie, come hell or high water. So we'll toss to see whether you ride to Leadville for a posse, or whether you stay here to watch the house while Johnnie and I ride to town."

The logic was clear. If they all three went to town for reinforcements, they might return to find the outlaws gone. It was six miles to Leadville, only an hour's lope each way. "Heads I go," Trevor said.

Gerry flipped the coin. "Heads it is, Tom. So off you go."

Trevor started toward the horses, then turned with a grin. "If I run into that Rand girl, Johnnie, I'll tell her you haven't soaked up any lead yet."

Harlan put in a dig of his own. "She'll sure be glad to hear that, Johnnie. She made me promise I wouldn't let anything happen to you."

"She doesn't give a damn what happens to me; or you either," Collier retorted. "Get going, Trevor."

But as Deputy Trevor disappeared into the trees it occurred to Collier that by this time the news of Murdy's murder would be known in Leadville. It would have been carried there by a stage driver on a night run over Mosquito Pass. The same driver would report that Harlan and Collier were trying to track the killers.

Angela Rand, keeping in close touch with the sheriff's office, would know about it by now. Tracking killers to a hide-out could mean a showdown gunfight with the law on the short end of the odds.

"She'll be frettin' her pretty head off," Gerry insisted, "until you show up hale and hearty— Hello, there's Buckshot Joe again."

Once more the man came out of the superintendent's house. This time he merely gathered an armload of cut firewood and returned inside.

Half an hour passed quietly. By now Trevor should have reached the stage road and turned down it toward Leadville. The next gulch which crossed the road would be California Gulch along which several of the Leadville smelters were located. Waiting in the cool shadows of the pines Collier's thoughts fastened on the county clerk's daughter. Her father wanted to pack her off to

Denver, to stop her from keeping company with a hunted man. Hunted not by the law but by outlaws. *Her dad's right,* John Collier admitted to himself. *So I'd better stay away from her.* It was the decent thing to do. Even if there was no risk, a man with a blank past who didn't know his own name had no business making love to a girl like Angela Rand.

"Look!" Harlan exclaimed suddenly. "Someone's coming!" He pointed not at the house but at the cart road leading upgulch to it. A horseman was riding at a canter toward the Mallory mine gate.

At the gate the man dismounted. He brought a key from his pocket and unlocked the padlock. After opening the gate he led his mount through it. "He doesn't look like a hideaway outlaw," Collier said. On the contrary the man gave the impression of a well-dressed townsman.

But clearly he had connections here; otherwise he wouldn't have a key to the gate. He wore a low-crowned hat and a brown whipcord riding suit. The face was ruddy, smooth-shaven and fairly young; Collier was sure he'd seen it before.

"Do you reckon he's Mr. Big, Gerry?"

Harlan shook his head. "He's not rich enough to be Mr. Big, Johnnie. A go-between messenger, likely. He's the guy that took a punch at Barry Holden the other day. A smoothie lawyer named Janford."

The name startled Collier. A scene in the

Clarendon dining room came back to him. Barry Holden twitting this man about banking a weekly jackpot of seven hundred dollars and getting punched in the chin for it.

They watched the lawyer ride on to the house. There he knocked at the front door which in a minute was opened to him. From his angle Collier couldn't see who let him in.

"He's one of them, all right," Harlan reasoned. "If he wasn't, they'd 've filled him full of lead by this time."

The lawyer was inside less than five minutes. When he came out he rode to the gate and through it, dismounting to relock the padlock. A moment later he was loping away downgulch.

"Let him go," Harlan decided. "We can pick him up in town. Right now we've got to keep an eye on the house."

"He brought 'em a payoff," Collier guessed.

"A payoff for what?"

"For getting rid of Murdy. It fits, Gerry. A stage driver brings in news of the Murdy killing. Yesterday Janford hears about it. So bright and early this morning he rides here with the blood money."

"Makes sense," Harlan admitted. "Guys like Gus Culp and Buckshot Joe don't work for nothing." He looked at his watch. "Tom oughta be more'n halfway to town by now."

Collier settled down to wait. The fireworks were sure to start when a posse arrived from Leadville.

# Thirteen

Trevor had been gone less than an hour when Buckshot Joe Wofford again came out of the house. The man disappeared into the barn. Since the barn stock had already been fed, he could be saddling up for a ride.

"He might get clean away," Harlan worried. "Tom's not even to town yet. It'll be an hour and a half before he can get help to us."

In a few minutes the rear door of the house opened and six armed men came out. The bearded man in the lead walked with a limp and was sure to be Gus Culp. "They're going somewhere, Gerry," Collier whispered. "They've got saddle rolls."

"They sure are, Johnnie. Looks like the whole caboodle of 'em are clearing out."

In a moment all seven outlaws were out of sight in the stable. Presumably Buckshot Joe had gone there first to saddle up.

"They're riding out on some devilment," Gerry was sure. "Likely that lawyer brought 'em a fresh order from Mr. Big."

"Either that," Collier countered, "or they're pulling out for good."

"Why would they quit here for good, Johnnie? They don't know we're on to 'em."

"Maybe Culp put two and two together. He

knows you and I and Trevor started tracking him from London Hill. He doesn't know how far we got before we lost the sign. But he *does* know what Janford told him just now."

"Which was what?"

"That on the way here he passed Trevor riding hard toward town. Trevor by himself. So Culp would know that you and I are still up the Weston Pass road somewhere. Why and where? Maybe watching at a rathole. Maybe waiting for Trevor to bring reinforcements."

"Could be," Harlan admitted. "Look. There they go." Seven mounted men filed out of the stable by its upgulch door. The door was left open, which would permit the dray team to walk out at will.

The seven mounted men each had a saddle pack and a rifle. They rode at a brisk pace up Iowa Gulch.

"They'll hole up at another hideaway somewhere and we've got to spot it," Harlan decided. "As soon as they're out of sight we'll track 'em. I'll leave a note for Tucker."

He tore a leaf from his notebook and scribbled in pencil.

Sheriff Tucker:
  Culp and six of his gang headed upgulch at ten a.m. Johnnie and I are tracking them. We'll avoid contact till you catch up.

*Harlan*

They walked back through the pines to the horses. Mounting there they rode to the claim gate, smashed the padlock with a rock and passed through.

At the superintendent's house Gerry tacked his message on the front door.

"No use pressing those guys too close, Johnnie. So we'll take time for a look inside."

The house doors were locked but one window latch wasn't. The deputies climbed through the window and found four disordered rooms. Empty liquor bottles lay about. Floors were unswept and kitchenware unwashed.

Harlan began going through drawers while Collier delved through the pockets of cast-off garments. "If we're lucky we might turn up a tip to who the payoff man is," Gerry said. "Messier than a pigpen, this joint. What those bums needed was a housekeeper."

"One of them tore up a letter," Collier said. Stooping, he began reclaiming from the floor trash fragments of a paper with writing on it. "Maybe they *did* have a housekeeper one time, Gerry. This looks like a woman's writing."

When he'd picked up all the fragments in sight he took them to a table and began fitting them together. "It's a note from some woman, all right," Collier concluded. "Her name's Ada and she wrote it to Gus Culp."

He joined together a few more pieces of the

puzzle. "Take a look, Gerry. Seems like she walked out on him back in July."

Harlan came from the bunk room and bent over the table. The note was dated July 13, a little more than a month before.

Gus:

When you get back you'll find me gone. I'll walk down to the stage road and catch a ride to town. By the time you read this I'll be on my way to San Francisco to file suit for divorce. You won't contest it because you won't dare tell a court who and where you are. And for my brother's sake, I won't either. Although he's a swindling blackmailer preying on a millionaire thief, he's still my brother. Good-bye,

*Ada*

Harlan gave a low whistle. "It fits Janford like the paper on the wall. Ada must be his sister."

"And she's Gus Culp's wife," Collier concluded. "Or was. We can ask the San Francisco police to look up the divorce records there."

Gerry Harlan made a copy of the message. Then he gathered up the torn pieces and put them in an envelope. "This'll sure build a fire under Janford. Let's start tracking, Johnnie."

They went out and mounted the horses. At the rear of the stable it was easy to pick up tracks of retreat. Seven mounted men had ridden up the gulch along a soft gravelly bank. At the upper end of the mining claim there was another padlocked gate. Again Harlan used a rock to smash it.

Above the gate the gulch narrowed. Slopes on either flank of it were heavily timbered. A pack trail led up the east side. A wagon would have been unable to pass here on account of boulders and log windfalls. "A few prospect pits up this gulch, but no mines," Gerry said. "It heads somewhere between Long's Hill and Ball Mountain."

Directly ahead of them the gulch curved to the east through a narrow, brushy defile.

The peak of a black hat showed over a boulder and Gerry yelled, "Hit the dirt, Johnnie."

He dived sideways from the saddle and landed in a sprawl by the trail. A length back of him Collier did the same. They'd been riding at the alert, rifles in hand. A shot cracked from the brushy bend and a bullet whistled. Collier rolled to a rock and lay flat behind it.

Gerry had crawled to a log windfall and was aiming over it. Two more shots came from the bend and Collier glimpsed a second hat. He triggered his rifle and the hat disappeared.

"They posted a rear guard," Gerry said, "in case anyone follows 'em. That guy you shot at is Buckshot Joe, Johnnie. Keep down. It's *you* they want, not me. Betcha there's at least ten thousand dollars on your head."

Peering over his rock for a target, Collier failed to see one. But he drew a shot and the bullet chipped sand into his face. He saw Gerry straighten up on his knees and pump three fast bullets. Return fire came from brush at the bend, although Collier saw only the tips of two rifle barrels there.

"A pair of 'em, Johnnie, and they've got us pinned down."

Collier saw red on Gerry's right sleeve. "Are you hit, Gerry?"

"In the arm," Harlan admitted. "Blast it! It's just bad enough to make me no good in a fight. I can't shoot worth shucks, left-handed. And there'll be more'n two of 'em potting at us if we stay here."

Collier couldn't doubt it. The five other outlaws might be less than a mile ahead. When they heard shooting by their rear guard they could turn back and join in.

"Like I told Trevor," Harlan said bitterly, "my job's to keep you alive, Johnnie. Nothin' to do but pull back while we can."

"I don't like running from those tramps," Collier protested. "Let's stick here and hold 'em off till the posse comes."

"Be at least an hour before they get here," Gerry calculated. "Culp'd have us chopped to pieces by that time. Running's not my style either. But there's a time to fight and a time to run. You're not more'n ten feet from the tree line, Johnnie. When I say roll, roll."

The two horses, reins hanging, had shied at the shooting and now stood just inside the trees on the gulch slope. It screened them from the outlaw firing.

"Roll, Johnnie!" Harlan, using his left hand, fired his six-gun toward the enemy to cover Collier. Collier rolled to another rock and from there crawled into the trees. Then he stood up angrily and began pumping bullets. "Do some rolling yourself, Gerry, while I pin 'em down."

With his right sleeve bloody, Gerry Harlan abandoned his rifle and rolled toward the tree line. Bullets plowed the gravel on either side of him. He arrived at the trees and crawled up the slope a little way, hatless and disheveled. John Collier helped him to his feet, handed him the reins of his horse. "Can you climb a saddle, Gerry?"

"Nothin' wrong with my legs, Johnnie." But the big deputy's face wore a pinch of pain as he got into the saddle. "Off we go, pardner, and keep in the trees."

They retreated along the wooded slope, well above the gulch bed. "Do you reckon they'll follow us, Gerry?"

"Not if they think a posse's on the way here. Their best bet's to keep going and lose themselves in the hills."

Presently the deputies came to an open gate and rode through it. Looking back, Collier saw no pursuit. He reined to a slower pace. "We better stop at the mine house and wrap up that arm."

Harlan shook his head. "Nope, we'll keep on till we clear the lower gate. You can't fight 'em by yourself, Johnnie."

They rode past the house and on through the lower gate. A mile below it they stopped at a waterhole in the gulch. There they dismounted to take off Gerry's coat and roll up his bloody sleeve.

"You'll find a bandage and some iodine in my saddlebag," Harlan said.

The arm was quickly bathed, treated and bandaged. Remounting, they rode on to the Weston Pass stage road.

When they were a mile down it in the direction of Leadville, Collier saw hard-riding men approaching uptrail. A wide, barrel-chested man in the lead looked like Sheriff Tucker.

"It's the posse all right," Gerry said. He spurred to meet them. "I see Tom Trevor with 'em; and Pete Loftus."

Several of the others proved to be townsmen hastily recruited. Tucker drew up, demanding sharply: "Why did you pull out, Gerry? Tom said you'd stick there and keep an eye on 'em."

"They rode upgulch," Harlan explained. "Johnnie and I followed a piece and then I got winged. If you ride fast you can pick up their tracks."

Tucker gave a curt nod to Trevor. "Get going, Tom. I'll catch up soon as I get the facts from Gerry."

Trevor, leading seven men, rode on at a gallop. Collier calculated that they'd be about an hour behind the retreating outlaws.

Gerry Harlan looked wistfully after them. "It oughta be a beaut of a fight. I sure hate to miss it."

"What you need," Tucker said, "is bed and a doctor. But first, give me a quick report."

"We've got the deadwood on that lawyer Janford," Gerry said. "He joined 'em at the mine house, either with a payoff or a message. After they took off upgulch, we found this." He showed the sheriff his copy of the torn-up note from Ada.

"Janford met us," Tucker said, "just before he got back to town. He told us he'd found Culp's hide-out and explained why he went there. It's a straight, logical story and he's got plenty to back it up."

Collier stared at the sheriff, surprised and incredulous. "How does he explain having a key to the gate padlock?"

"It's simple," Tucker said. "The mine's in litigation and Janford's the lawyer for one of the litigants. Pending a decision they gave him the job of posting a caretaker there. It was all in the Leadville *Chronicle* a month or so ago. A man named Rusk applied for the caretaker job and Janford hired him. Gave him a key to the gate padlock and kept a duplicate himself. Both sets of litigants knew about it, including Mallory. Honest as daylight, Lou Mallory is. Like I said, it was all in the papers."

"But what about Janford hiring a crooked caretaker?" Harlan argued. "Rusk, he calls the guy. But his description matches Gil Hocker's."

"Likely he *was* Hocker," Tucker conceded, "using the name Rusk. But how could Janford know that? I didn't recognize Hocker myself till I remembered seeing his mug on a Wanted poster from Arizona. How could Janford know the man only took the caretaker job to use the mine for a gang hide-out?"

"Janford went to see them there," Collier said.

"Yes, and he told us why. The first month went by and the caretaker didn't come to town for his second month's pay. So Janford got to wondering if he was still on the job. This morning he rode out to see. The man who let him in wasn't Rusk. Janford says he was a skinny guy he'd never seen before. The skinny guy said Rusk was off hunting meat. But he looked tough and Janford got suspicious. The place looked like a lot of men had been drinking liquor there. Janford says he had a feeling of being watched from a back room and it scared him stiff. So he got out of there and hit for town. On the way he ran into my posse and told us all about it; said he figured it was the Culp gang hiding out there."

Collier wasn't convinced and it was plain that Harlan wasn't either. Since the posse would soon have found it out anyway, the lawyer had nothing to lose by telling it first. "What about this note from Ada?"

Tucker looked again at the copy made by Harlan. "It proves Culp's wife was there with them, up till a month ago. She quit him and went to the West Coast for a divorce. A crooked brother of hers ties in somewhere. But she doesn't mention his name or say he's a lawyer. She just calls him a slick blackmailer. Leadville's full of bunco men and slickers. Nothing to show that this one's Mel Janford."

"He banks seven hundred a week, according to Barry Holden. Where does he get it?"

"I asked him about that, right after he punched Holden. He says it's a five-thousand-dollar law fee he earned, payable in weekly payments. Last week he collected the final installment."

Again Collier and Harlan exchanged skeptical looks. Law fees were usually paid by check and the weekly deposits had been made with cash. "Did you ask who his client was?"

The sheriff lighted a stogie, puffed it complaisantly, then nodded. "No secret about it. The client was Louis Mallory. Janford says he earned it by representing Mallory in the mine litigation. Not only that, but I checked with Mallory himself. He admits he paid Janford that fee in just that way."

"Which nominates Mallory for the millionaire thief," Collier concluded, "mentioned by Ada."

"Wrong again," Tucker corrected with an indulgent smile. "I'd bet my badge that Lou Mallory never stole a penny. What's more, he's no millionaire. Fact is he's scraping mud bottom and if he loses this suit he'll be stony broke." The sheriff puffed his stogie and blew a neat smoke ring. "So you've got no case against Janford, boys. Or Mallory either." He looked critically at Harlan's arm. "Better take him home and put him to bed, Collier. Then call in Doc Fowler. Me, I've got to overtake my posse."

He went loping up the road.

The two deputies gazed after him with frustrated stares, then took the opposite direction, toward Leadville.

They were within sight of August Meyer's smelter on the far bank of California Gulch before either of them spoke. "Slippery as an eel, that guy!" Harlan said finally.

It was clear that he meant Janford.

# Fourteen

Doctor Fowler called promptly at the Clarendon's room 278. "Can't you boys stay out of fights?" he complained after treating and dressing Gerry's arm. "It's only a flesh wound. You won't need a sling. But stay in bed till tomorrow morning, Gerry. That's an order. And Collier, right after supper give him this opiate pill. I want him to sleep like a baby all night."

When he was gone Collier locked the door and took a nap himself. Every bone ached, for the circuit they'd ridden via Mosquito and Weston passes made more than sixty rough miles.

Shortly after sundown a waiter brought supper on a tray.

While they were eating, Barry Holden came in. His face had a rosy excitement and this evening's *Chronicle* was in his hand. "The town's jumpin'!" Barry grinned. "Best story I've had since the six-man gunfight at the Odeon, last month. Take a look."

He tossed the paper to Collier who saw tall headlines: CULP CORNERED; DOWNS DEPUTY and ESCAPES; MELEE at the MALLORY MINE. It was a hard and fast rule at the *Chronicle* that every important headline must be an alliteration.

On their way up Harrison Avenue to the Clarendon at noon, Harlan and Collier had stopped at the county attorney's office to make a brief report. They'd given him a copy of the note signed "Ada." But as he read the news story Collier saw many details which they hadn't bothered to mention.

"Is Tucker's posse back yet?" he asked.

"Not yet," the reporter said. "They'll likely be chasing those outlaws all night and tomorrow."

"Then where did you get all this stuff I didn't know myself? Like one of the outlaws wearing a black and white turtleneck sweater?"

"It was the skinny guy who wore the sweater," Holden said. "The one who let Janford in. Janford told his story to Tucker on the way to town. When he got here he went straight to the *Chronicle* and told it again. Since then he's been breasting the Grand Hotel bar with forty men trying to buy him a drink. Everybody in town's heard his yarn by now."

Harlan snorted. "The same song and dance he gave Tucker on the road! A pack of lies from start to finish, if you ask me."

Holden whipped out a notebook. "May I quote you on that, Gerry?"

Before Harlan could assent, Collier stopped him. "Let's let him think we believe him. Give him enough rope and he may trip himself. Nothing to gain by calling him a liar till we can prove it."

The reporter put away his notebook and ruefully rubbed a sore chin. "It still hurts, where he socked me. I'd sure like to see that fella scuttled. But most everyone believes him, including the county attorney. His story seems to check out."

Collier hesitated a minute, then asked, "What does Angela Rand think?"

"Haven't seen Angela yet. She must have read the evening paper by now. Bet she can hardly wait to get the lowdown from you, Johnnie Collier. But her pappy's ridin' close herd on her. Wants her to keep her nose out of this; wants to pack her off to an aunt in Denver. Won't hardly let her out of the house except to go to work with him."

"What else does the paper say?" Harlan asked.

Collier read down the column. "Says the county attorney has telegraphed the San Francisco police. Wants them to check divorce actions there for the case of Ada versus Gus Culp. Asks them to find Ada and get her maiden name."

"Her maiden name," Barry reminded them, "would be her brother's name. Which would tip us to the swindling blackmailer mentioned in her note."

"No answer yet?"

"Not yet, Gerry. Ought to be one by morning. If it comes in I'll let you know."

The reporter stayed half an hour longer, drawing the deputies out about the killing of

Murdy at the London Hill stage station and the tracking of the killers to Iowa Gulch via Weston Pass. When he'd pumped them dry, Barry hurried away to write another story.

A pill on the table reminded Collier of the doctor's orders. He handed it to Harlan with a glass of water. "Your dessert, pardner." The big deputy had been sitting up in bed with a supper tray across his knees. Collier took the tray away. "I'll turn in myself soon as I finish reading the news."

With his boots propped on a table and his chair tilted back, Collier read column after column of the *Chronicle*. In addition to a complete coverage of today's story, there were lengthy speculations about the mystery of John Collier.

When will he remember? Tomorrow? Next week? Next month? Or will he *ever* be able to tell us who he is, where he came from, and why?

There were quotes from an authoritative book on amnesia written by a Boston specialist. "Sometimes," Collier read, "a victim's memory returns piecemeal, sometimes all at once."

Editorially the paper said:

We have no faint idea which of our citizens has been persistently trying to bring about young Collier's demise. But we feel sure that

that evil person is on pins and needles right now. For presumably his guilt will be exposed when and if John Collier is able to look back over his life. We think the county should double the guard over Collier. Only by keeping him alive can we hope to learn the truth.

Here in Leadville this was the story of the hour and the *Chronicle* was playing it to the hilt. There was a puzzled treatment of two accusing words in Ada's note: "millionaire thief."

Which thief? And which millionaire? The term has been bandied loosely around Leadville. It has been estimated that forty-six of our citizens are either already millionaires, or own silver mines which will make them millionaires in the course of the year. Perhaps the woman Ada meant one of those forty-six; or perhaps she merely used the word rhetorically. She could judge only by the amount of hush money the man has been paying to her scalawag brother, and to others.

Let us hasten to absolve four of our wealthiest neighbors, Mr. Tabor, Mr. Meyer, Mr. Werner and Mr. Hammond. We cannot conceive of any of those estimable gentlemen dealing with the likes of Gus Culp, garroter and stage robber, or paying out blood money for the lives of Frank Bryson and John Collier. Our hope is that the matter will be settled in short order by the return of Collier's memory. When he is able to point out Ada's "millionaire thief" and her equally despicable brother, no one will cheer louder than the *Chronicle*.

When Collier finished reading he looked up to see Gerry Harlan sound asleep.

He laid the paper aside. Because of his afternoon nap Collier himself wasn't in the least sleepy. It wasn't quite nine o'clock and Harrison Avenue, below his window, was alive with clacking wheels and voices. He wondered what Angela was doing now. She would have read the very news items and comment he'd just read himself. What would she think of the note signed Ada? As a woman would she draw from it some meaning or conclusion more subtle than anything which had occurred to Collier or to Sheriff Tucker? A remark of Barry Holden's came back to Collier. "Bet she can hardly wait to get the lowdown from *you*, Johnnie."

A compelling urge to talk it over with her possessed Collier. It was only a five-minute walk to her house. If he went there alone he'd be breaking every rule of safety and of common sense. He'd been shot at, even with Gerry siding him, on his last walk from that house.

Yet desperately he wanted to see Angela tonight, even if only for a minute. Her father was bent on sending her to Denver and in the end was likely to have his way. He might put her on a coach tomorrow for one of the track ends. In which case John Collier might never see her again.

His last chance could be tonight. He looked at the sleeping Harlan and knew that the big deputy, if awake, would never consent to his going alone. And even if Gerry went along he'd be little good as a guard tonight, with his shooting arm bandaged.

There really wasn't much risk, Collier's mind argued, if he went alone. Last time his call had been advertised in advance. This time no one would know he was going there. And tonight Culp's gang, or most of them, were aflight through the hills with a posse at their heels.

He needn't go through the lobby. There were back stairs leading to a side street. It would keep him off Harrison. He could detour up to Poplar which was dark and entirely residential, and so get to the Rand house unseen.

John Collier brushed his hair and put on a tie. He took off his gunbelt but wedged the gun itself under the narrow dress belt with the skirt of his coat hiding it. He'd be foolhardy to go out unarmed. Yet if he wore a cartridge belt he'd be the more easily recognized in darkness. For the same reason he put on Gerry's hat instead of his own. His own was tall-crowned with a bullet hole through it. Gerry's had a flat crown and was black.

He blew out the oil lamp, unlocked the door and put the key in his pocket. Stepping into a deserted hallway he closed the door softly. Should he relock it? He decided not to. There was no second key and Gerry shouldn't be locked in. The killers weren't after Harlan; the man with a price on his head was John Collier.

The hall had a deep carpet and Collier made no sound as he hurried down the north wing to back stairs. He descended them to a side street where only a few windows showed light. Pulling the low-crowned black hat over his eyes he hurried past the *Herald* office, then past the ticket office of the South Park Stage Company. Beyond there everything was dark to Poplar Street.

Turning up Poplar Collier passed the house where Lola Loomis lived. In the block beyond he stopped for a moment, gazing quizzically across at a cottage belonging to a lawyer named Gentry. It had been pointed out to him by Tucker as the trap where on his first day in Leadville he'd been slugged unconscious. Collier had no memory of that mishap but he knew it was true. Lola herself had directed him there. Tire tracks of a spring wagon had been found in the back yard.

The man in the flat black hat moved on past other cottages and cabins, all dark. In the northernmost block of the town the street rose steeply to an eminence called Capitol Hill. There Collier found himself directly back of the imposing Meyer mansion where all three floors were lighted. The place had an acre of landscaped lawn with a cast-iron fence around it. Tonight a dozen parked carriages meant that a party was going on.

Circling to its front side Collier saw that the Rand house, across from it, had only one lighted window. It was the parlor window and beyond the glow of it he saw Angela's silhouette. She was reading a newspaper. As Collier clicked the gate latch she moved promptly toward the door as though expecting someone.

John Collier didn't have to knock. As he stepped onto the porch the door opened and there she stood, lovely in her surprise at the sight of him. "Oh! I thought it was Dad coming home! I've been dying to see you, Johnnie Collier. But where is . . . ?"

Alarm clouded her face when she saw that Gerry Harlan wasn't with him. Collier stepped into the hall and closed the door. "Don't worry. Nobody knows I came. Gerry's asleep and I didn't want to wake him. I just *had* to see you a minute, Angela."

"But you shouldn't have come alone!"

"I didn't." He drew back the skirt of his coat a little to let her see the gun.

She led him into the parlor and pulled down the window blinds. To make sure his shadow wouldn't be thrown on a shade, she seated him in a chair not in line with the lamp. "Dad imagines an assassin behind every tree, waiting to shoot at you."

"But not tonight," Collier assured her. "They think I'm home asleep with the door locked and Gerry there with me."

"Tell me about Iowa Gulch," she said eagerly, "and the note from Ada. Did the paper print it right?"

"They didn't leave out anything," he told her, "except the way Janford looked when he left the house. He claims he was scared stiff. But he didn't look scared to me. He took time to relock the gate padlock. A scared man would ride right through and keep on going lickety-split."

"I've never trusted Mel Janford. But Dad thinks I'm unfair to him. Everyone says he's a good title lawyer."

"You say your father's out tonight?"

"Yes, Johnnie." She looked at him with a half-shy smile. "That's what Gerry calls you, isn't it?"

"It sounds a lot better when you say it."

"Dad and Raymond Otis," the girl said, "are working late at the office. We've been swamped the last few days. Dad had to put on an extra copy clerk. Lola Loomis is helping out this week too. It's a chance for her to earn a little extra money before school begins."

At Collier's questioning look she explained: "The secret's out about this year's Ledger B being destroyed. Hundreds of titles were recorded in it. Many of those owners are speculators who want to sell their property or borrow money on it. But a buyer or lender is sure to demand an abstract of title from the county records."

Collier nodded. Such properties would need to be re-recorded in another ledger. "And they all want to do it at once?"

"The speculators do. Owners with no need to sell or borrow aren't in any particular hurry. They have receipts from the county clerk to prove that their titles were put on record earlier in the year."

"What's your slant on the woman Ada?"

"I don't think she went to San Francisco, like it says in the note."

"You don't? Why?"

"She wouldn't tell them where she was really going," Angela said. "They're murderers and she's afraid of them. She knows they kill people who can tell tales on them. I think she said San Francisco to throw them off the track. She'd be safer to go in some other direction—like to Santa Fe or New Orleans or Chicago."

Collier pondered it. The note said she was sure Culp wouldn't contest her divorce petition because as a wanted outlaw he wouldn't dare make contact with a court. That would be true regardless of where she filed the suit.

"We'll know tomorrow, Angela, when we get an answer from the San Francisco police."

Again the girl demurred. "I don't think so, Johnnie. In the petition she must use her correct name and it's not likely to be Culp."

It took a minute for Collier to catch the logic of it. Then he could only agree. If Culp had married Ada before he became a widely known outlaw, he'd probably married her under the name he was born with. A name other than Culp. And that would be the woman's name of record, under which she must request her divorce.

"What's this I hear about your dad sending you to Denver?"

"He wants to. But I'm not going." Angela's face took a stubborn set. "I was twenty-one in June and I won't be treated like a child."

"You can't blame him," Collier said. "A slug with my name on it could easy hit whoever I'm with. So I guess I'd better swear off seeing you— which won't be easy." In a moment he added brightly: "No danger tonight, though; Culp and most of his outfit are high-tailing through the hills."

"Let's hope so, Johnnie. But Dad would be furious if he knew you were here. He insists I must never see you again until . . ."

"Until Mr. Big and everyone working for him,"

Collier broke in, "are dead or in jail." He reached for his hat. The color and shape of it reminded him of Gerry Harlan. "So I'd better be going. Gerry'll raise hob if he wakes up and finds me gone."

"I'm so glad you came," Angela said warmly. "The first chance we get Lola and I'll take lunch at the Clarendon and perhaps you and Gerry can join us."

She went out into the reception hall with him. "Good night, Johnnie."

"Good night; and please don't go to Denver till I see you again."

"I'm not going at all," she promised. "Although Lola thinks Dad's right. She says if I go to Denver she'll go with me and stay a week or so. It would give her a chance to do some shopping there before her school starts here."

"You gals'd have a right good time," Collier said.

Before he could open the door they heard hoofbeats and wheels in the street. A cab was pulling up in front.

"It's Dad coming home!" Angela said in dismay.

"Look, Angela, I don't want you quarreling with him. So maybe he'd better not see me leave."

She took his arm. "Come. I'll let you out the back door."

They passed through a dark dining room and kitchen to a rear exit. In the gloom there the outline of her face seemed lovelier than ever. "If I knew my own name," Collier said, "I'd ask to kiss you good night."

"A girl on a balcony once said, 'What's in a name?'" The whisper was so faint that John Collier might have missed it.

But he didn't. So he took her cheeks between his hands and felt the warmness of her lips. Then she opened the door for him and he was gone.

# Fifteen

He circled the house and reached the street in time to hail the same hack which had brought Milton Rand home. He got into it and said, "The *Herald* office, please."

The cabman trotted his team down the hill to the upper end of Harrison. At a narrow side street he turned left, passing between the Clarendon Hotel and the nearly finished Tabor Opera House. Just beyond the rear of the Clarendon he stopped in front of the *Chronicle*'s competitor, the *Daily Herald.*

Collier waited till the cab rolled away before retreating a few paces to a stairway entrance leading to a second-floor corridor of the Clarendon. A minute later he was up the steps and hastening along that corridor to his room.

Would Gerry still be asleep? Collier slipped quietly into 278 and in the room's darkness could hear his friend's deep even breathing from the bed. He locked the door, then groped for the lamp and lighted it.

Yes, Gerry was soundly sleeping. Apparently he hadn't moved during the hour of Collier's absence. Collier took off the flat black hat and propped it in a position to keep lamplight from disturbing the sleeper. Then he took off his coat and pulled the forty-five gun from his belt.

He was about to lay the gun on the table when he saw a pair of boots which weren't either his own or Harlan's. Or rather he saw only the toes of the boots showing beneath a curtain hung obliquely across a corner of the room where it made a triangular closet.

With a shock John Collier realized that a man stood back of the curtain. A man waiting to kill him as soon as it could be done with little or no outcry! He would expect Collier to undress at once, blow out the lamp and get in bed with Harlan.

Garroting, people said, had been a common method of murder for the Culp gang of footpads which had terrorized Leadville last winter and spring. And how easy it would be for this one! He could plan to strangle Collier in his sleep without awaking Harlan. And even if there were an out-cry, an armed killer would have all the advantage.

The bald logic of it came in a flash to Collier

and made him keep the gun in his hand. He faced the curtain with it and challenged, "Come on out!"

A slight quiver of the curtain meant that the intruder now knew for the first time that it was he who was trapped, not Collier. But the boot toes didn't move and there was no answer.

"Your boots need a shine," Collier said.

This time one of the boots disappeared and the movement caused the tinkle of a spur.

"Shall I shoot through the curtain? Or would you rather step out for an even break?" After this second challenge Collier moved a quiet step to one side so that his voice wouldn't guide a bullet.

There was a breathless wait. Then the curtain was swept aside and the man came out shooting.

His first shot beat Collier's. Aimed at where a voice had been it passed to the left of the shifting speaker. The man's hulking, stoop-shouldered build and round hairy face seemed oddly familiar. John Collier squeezed his own trigger a split second before the man fired again.

It made three shots all spaced in a breath of time. The sound and smoke choked the closeness of the room. A hundred people in the hotel must have heard them. The roars chopped into the sleeping consciousness of Gerry Harlan and brought him with a jump from the bed. He stood in his underwear, blinking at a man on the floor and at Johnnie Collier.

"It's over, Gerry," Collier said. The man with

the round hairy face had collapsed at his feet with a chest hit.

A hubbub of questions came from the corridors and there were shouts from the lobby below. Harlan looked blankly at his roommate. "How the devil did he get in?" he demanded.

"He just walked in, Gerry. I went out for a while and left the door unlocked. When I got back he was laying for me."

"Who is he, Johnnie?"

"His name's Kansas." The odd promptness of Collier's answer didn't at once impress either of them.

Gerry picked up the man's gun and saw that it had been fired twice. Collier's had been fired only once. Belatedly a question formed in Gerry Harlan's eyes. He gazed closely at the dying man's face, then quizzically at his roommate.

"You're right, Johnnie. He's Rufe Kansas. Last spring we had him in jail on a holdup charge. Then he jumped bail and disappeared. *But how did you know it?*"

"I didn't," Collier said.

"Then how the heck did you know his name's Kansas?"

John Collier laid his gun aside and sat down on the bed. A storm of talk came from the hall and someone pounded on the door. Harlan opened it and Proprietor Bush came in, harassed, indignant, confused. "You mean another killer got in here?" he demanded. "Thank God he didn't get you, Mr. Collier. Who is he?"

"A Culp gunnie," Harlan said, "by the name of Rufe Kansas." Others crowded in from the hall and one of them was Constable Monte Murray.

Murray kneeled for a moment by the man on the floor. "The guy's dead," he reported. "He's Rufe Kansas, all right. You did a good job outgunning him, Gerry."

"It wasn't me," Harlan said. "I was asleep. Johnnie Collier out-triggered him. You haven't answered me yet, Johnnie. How did you know his name's Kansas?"

Collier ran a hand through his hair, rumpling it. "I just knew, Gerry. Maybe it was the sudden shock of seeing him—that ugly, black-stubbled face of his popping out from behind a curtain. Right away I remembered the other time."

"What other time?"

"I was in a parlor that had a brick fireplace," Collier said. "There was cut firewood stacked on the hearth and a man with a round, black-stubbled face picked up a stick of it. Another man was punching me in the back with a gun. He said, 'Put him to sleep, Kansas.' Then the man with the stick of firewood hit me with it. The next I knew I was riding in a hack with Doctor Fowler and Cal Barstow. They brought me to this room and told me I'd been picked up from a wagon wreck on Chestnut Street."

Harlan gave a low, soft whistle. His eyes shifted to Monte Murray's and both officers nodded.

"That room with a brick fireplace," the constable said, "is in Lawyer Gentry's cottage on Poplar."

Harlan added: "It's the last thing that happened to you, Johnnie, before your memory put on blinders. What else can you remember from that parlor?"

"Not a thing," Collier said.

"Who was it punched a gun in your back?"

"I don't know."

"How did they get you there?"

"I don't know."

"Did you see Gil Hocker? It was him who drove you away in a wagon."

"All I saw was the man in front of me. The man who hit me. This one." Collier, still sitting on the bed, stared down at the dead Rufe Kansas.

Bush called in two of his porters. "Pick him up and get him out of here," he commanded. "Take this rug out and fetch in another one."

As the dead man and the stained rug were being carried out, the hotel man looked reproachfully at Constable Murray. "I'm trying to run a respectable hotel for respectable people. Can't you keep hoodlums out of it? What kind of a police force are you, anyway?"

The answer came sharply from a small, thin, nervous man who elbowed his way into the room. He was City Marshal Duggan. "We're doing our best, Mr. Bush. Everybody get out of here except me and Collier and Harlan and Murray and Mr. Bush."

When the onlookers had been herded out he closed the door. "Okay," he barked. "What happened?"

"I took a walk," Collier said, "and the man was in here when I got back."

"A walk? Where?"

Embroiling Angela Rand wouldn't help any. She'd concealed the fact of a caller from her father and it was best to leave it that way. "Up the street a piece," Collier evaded. "No one saw me. I left by the back stairs and returned the same way."

That was his story and he stood pat on it. But a narrow-eyed stare from Harlan suggested that Gerry was making a shrewdly correct guess.

Duggan fumed and sputtered and paced the room. "You broke all the rules, Collier. How can we protect you unless you cooperate?"

Again there was a knock and this time Harlan admitted Doctor Fowler. He came in briskly with his medical satchel. "Anybody need patching up?" he inquired. "I hear you've had another gunfight, Collier."

"He's not even scratched," Harlan said. "Fact is it even jarred a small chunk of his memory back. He recollects the last thing that happened before he got conked in the lawyer's house."

"Does that make sense, Doctor?" Collier asked. "The paper tonight had a piece along on that line."

"I read it myself," Fowler said, "and it's substantially correct. Sometimes an amnesia victim gets his memory back all at once, sometimes bit by bit. What happened to you is a good omen, young man. Tomorrow you may remember something else; and eventually, everything. Well, since there are no new gunshot wounds in here, I'll be running along. Good night, gentlemen." The doctor took a brisk departure.

A new nervousness gripped Duggan. "Look," he insisted, "let's keep it quiet about Collier rememberin' Rufe Kansas' name. If it gets out, the man who hired Rufe'll hear about it. It'll put him in a squeeze and he'll double the price on your head, Collier."

The logic was sound and no one argued with it. It had been assumed all along that the complete return of Collier's memory would explain the murder of Frank Bryson, as well as all the attempts on Collier's life and identify the man back of them. And since a fragment of that lost memory had returned, the man must expect other fragments to return either in slow or swift order. Certainly it would speed up his race to destroy John Collier.

"Trouble is we're too late," Gerry Harlan reminded them. "We had a nosy crowd in here a few minutes ago, and more out in the hall. They heard Johnnie tell about Rufe Kansas and his stick of firewood. By morning it'll be all over town."

Again Duggan paced the room, stewing and fretting. "Then we'll have to double the guard. Look, Mr. Bush. Is the next room vacant?" He thumbed toward an interior door through which Murdy had once tried to force an entry.

"If it's not," the hotel man said, "I'll vacate it at once."

The city marshal whipped around toward his constable. "Okay, Monte, pack a bag and move in there. Whenever Harlan's asleep, you spell him. I want one of you awake day and night with an eye on Collier. When he goes down to the dining room, or out on the street, I want one of you on either side of him. Sheriff Tucker'll back me up. Understand? If money can buy bullets, they'll be shooting from all angles after this."

"Okay," Murray said. "I'll go down and register right now. Mr. Bush, let me know when 276 is ready and I'll move in. And I'll need a key to the connecting door."

Monte Murray left the room and presently Bush followed him with Duggan.

When they were alone Harlan turned sternly to his roommate. "You messed things up, Johnnie; sneaking off to call on your girl."

Collier retorted, "You're just sore because you didn't get to see Lola."

"All right," the big deputy said grudgingly. "I

won't peach on you. But don't let it happen again."

"I won't," Collier promised. "Not unless I take you along with me."

"Me and Murray both," Harlan insisted. "From here on you'll be a sitting duck, day and night."

# Sixteen

At eight in the morning a hack left the Rand house on Capitol Hill. It rattled down Harrison with Milton Rand and his daughter in it. "Another few days and we'll be caught up," the county clerk said.

"I hope so, Dad." Angela gave the answer absently because her mind was on something else.

All night she'd been thinking about a note signed Ada and a new possibility had occurred to her. She was impatient to follow through on it and intended to do so at the first opportunity.

"I hear that Collier boy's back in town," Rand said. "I want you to keep away from him."

"If he asks to come to see me, I'll say no," the girl promised. But she had a feeling that when Johnnie wanted to see her he'd come without asking. So far her father had no suspicion about last night's call.

"If I catch you with him," Rand decreed

brusquely, "off you'll go to Denver even if I have to take you there myself."

As the hack neared the Clarendon excited talk reached them from the sidewalks and they heard the name Collier. "Looks like that Collier boy don't need no bodyguard," a man said, "the way he out-triggered another killer last night."

Milton Rand caught the sense of it and made the hack stop. Getting out he joined the sidewalk crowd and asked a few questions. Then he got back into the cab and made it drive on. "That does it, Angela. The damned fool took a walk last night while his guard was asleep. When he got back a man hiding in the room shot at him. Came off second best, though; the cowboy downed him."

"You're sure he's safe?" Angela asked breathlessly.

"This time he is. But he can't always have luck like that. They'll get him next time—and maybe whoever happens to be with him."

At the lower end of Harrison they dismissed the hack and went into the county clerk's offices. Ray Otis, in shirt sleeves and with a green shade over his eyes, was already at work there. So were two temporary helpers, Lola Loomis and a shabby oldster named McClure.

Otis looked up from his ledger. "There'll be a meeting of the county commissioners at nine o'clock, Mr. Rand. They ask that you attend."

The routine of work got quickly under way.

181

Rand went into his small inner office. In the main office Angela sat at one desk and Otis at another, each to record titles in a ledger. Angela recorded new titles and Otis re-recorded deeds and patents which, except for the recent burning of 1879 Book B, would already have been on record. Lola Loomis sat apart in a quiet, curtained alcove where she checked the copyings of yesterday against the deeds themselves, to make sure the copiers hadn't erred in a name or number. Once they were checked, she handed each title to McClure who put it in an envelope with a receipt, then penned a letter to the owner notifying him that he could pick up the paper at his convenience.

At nine o'clock Milton Rand left for the council room to attend a meeting of the commissioners. The instant he was gone Angela hurried to Lola's alcove with a confidence. "I'm going up to the *Chronicle* office, Lola. They keep a file of the *Rocky Mountain News* and I want to look at every issue since July fifteenth."

"Why?" Lola asked. The *News* was the leading daily paper at Denver.

"Every day they run a vital statistics column. Births, deaths, marriages and petitions for divorce. Maybe I'll see mention of Ada's."

"But she went to San Francisco."

"Or in the opposite direction so she wouldn't be followed. The nearest city in the opposite direction, where she could get a good divorce lawyer and live comfortably while waiting, is Denver. If she's there, she arrived about July fifteenth, forty days ago."

"But isn't the residence requirement longer than that?" Lola wondered.

"Probably. But we don't know what she told her lawyer. If she told him she'd lived there six months he'd have no reason to doubt her. He'd make the petition promptly to get things started. She knows her husband won't appear to contest it or to raise a technicality, so she could hope to get the decree by default."

"Suppose she *is* in Denver. What then?"

"I'll become an obedient daughter, Lola, and go there myself. Remember, you promised to go with me. We can . . . Sh! Here comes Mr. McClure."

It was only a five-minute walk to the *Chronicle* and by half past nine Angela was poring over news files there. Recent issues of the *Rocky Mountain News* were racked in a room open to the public. Angela looked first at the last fifteen days of July, scanning only the vital statistics column.

What she wanted wasn't there and with her hope dimming a little Angela took down issues for the current month, August. On some days no divorce petitions had been made. On other days there'd been as many as three. Angela didn't expect to find the name Culp. All she looked for was the name Ada. An outlaw would be likely to live under an alias but his wife would keep her own given name.

In the issue for August 17, only eight days ago, Angela found it. A divorce application filed that day was described as "Ada Milligan versus Augustus Milligan." No address was given, nor the name of Ada's lawyer.

Angela hurried back to her father's offices, confident that she'd guessed right. The names Ada and Augustus could hardly be a coincidence. Leaving here on July 13, Ada could have been in Denver a little more than a month before hunting up a lawyer. Now she'd be awaiting the outcome at some quiet boarding-house or hotel. Finding her shouldn't be too difficult. She would have been required to leave an address at which she could be notified when to appear in court.

Milton Rand wasn't yet back from the county meeting. Vivid with excitement, Angela joined Lola in the curtained alcove. "She's in Denver, Lola! And we're going there to see her."

Lola was quite willing. It would be fun riding a stage and train there with Angela and she needed a shopping vacation before school started next month. They could see a show or two together. "But Angela, why do you think she'll tell on her husband? Her note said she wouldn't."

"The first thing we want to know," Angela said,

"is whether she's Mel Janford's sister. If she is, there'll be a family resemblance. There nearly always is between brother and sister. Her own face will give Janford away."

"And then?"

"Once she knows we've got the goods on her brother, she'll no longer have any reason to protect her husband; or the man who pays her husband. Remember the way her note ended: 'And for my brother's sake, I won't tell either. Although he's a so-and-so, he's still my brother.'"

"True," Lola agreed. "She's sure to be reading the Leadville papers. You can buy them in Denver. She'll see her own note published in yesterday's *Chronicle*; and learn that her brother was seen calling at the Iowa Gulch hide-out."

"That should panic her," Angela concluded. "Or at least soften her up. When we convince her that her brother's trapped, she's almost sure to break down and tell us who's footing the bills and why. But listen, Lola! Not a word of this to anyone. If Dad knew what I'm up to, he wouldn't let me go. I mean he'd send me somewhere else than to Denver. Tracking down murderers is the last thing he wants me to do."

"Can't we tell Gerry Harlan and John Collier?"

"Definitely no," Angela said firmly. "They'd be against our going because they'd think we might get ourselves into trouble. We'll tell no one at all until we've wormed what we can out of

Ada. If she names the chief criminal here at Leadville, we can tell the Denver police."

"Are these ready for me, Miss Loomis?" The shabby oldster, McClure, appeared with a wicker basket to collect whatever titles Lola had checked against their ledger copies.

"This pile is," Lola said, "and this one isn't."

An entrance and a voice in the main office told Angela that her father was back. His words, "Where's my daughter?" sounded angry.

When she went out to meet him, a curt jerk of his thumb summoned her to the privacy of his inner office. "You had a caller last night," he charged. "It was that cowboy who gets shot at wherever he goes. I told you not to see him."

"He knocked at the door. I wasn't expecting him. It would have been rude not to let him in."

"Why didn't you tell me?"

"I didn't want to upset you," Angela said.

"A hackman let it out," Milton Rand told her bitterly. "A hackman who hauled him back to his hotel. A man was waiting there to shoot him—a killer who might just as easily have followed him to my parlor. I've had enough of this, Angela; so I'm booking you to Denver on the first stage I can buy space on."

The girl made herself look contrite and dutiful. "I suppose you know best, Dad. I'll go. Today if you like. Lola says she'll go with me."

Surprise at her sudden surrender took the

bluster out of Rand. He stared for a moment, then spoke calmly. "Let's reserve seats for you at once. I'm told the South Park Line coaches are booked a solid week in advance. But maybe we can get you on the Canon City line tonight or tomorrow. Come along."

He took her out to a cab and they rode up Harrison to the Barlow and Sanderson ticket office. "I think we'd be more comfortable on the Canon City line," Angela said.

"It's longer," Milton Rand said, "but it has no mountain passes. A water grade all the way." The route would take them a hundred and ten miles down the Arkansas River to the D & R G track-end at Canon City, from which they could ride a train to Denver via Colorado Springs.

At the stage office a ticket clerk looked up bookings. "I can let you have two reservations for tomorrow night, Mr. Rand. Nothing sooner. The coach leaves at six p.m. It's an all-night and all-day run to Canon City, with a good train connection there."

"We'll take them." Milton Rand paid for the tickets and handed them to his daughter. "The two of you," he said, "can start packing."

# Seventeen

John Collier, flanked by Harlan and Murray, went hopefully into the Clarendon dining room. It was a little past noon and the room was nearly full. His eyes flicked from table to table and then showed disappointment.

"I was hoping the same thing," Gerry said.

"What?"

"That maybe Lola and Angela'd show up. Looks like we're out of luck."

As they took a four-chair table, others looked at them with a lively interest. All three men carried forty-fives and everybody knew why. Last night's would-be killer could easily be replaced. More than likely he'd already been replaced and right now some new assassin was watching for his chance. For everyone knew that John Collier in the shock of a gunfight had reopened one of the darkened windows of his memory. And no one would know it better, or fear it more, than the man who most wanted Collier dead.

"He'll up the ante," one diner remarked to another, "and his guns'll take bigger chances than ever."

Monte Murray, after a quick survey of the room,

relaxed a little. "Everybody in here looks okay, Gerry."

"You can't always tell by looks," Harlan argued. "Take that guy in a plaid suit with his hair parted in the middle. You'd think maybe he was a shoe salesman. But he's Jock Henderson of Abilene. Used to be a Kansas town tamer and they say he killed nine men in the line of duty. It was one too many so they fired him. Right now he's a gun guard at a mine on Fryer Hill."

Whatever the price on John Collier's head, it would need a reckless assassin to try for a kill in here. Harlan and Murray sat on either side of Collier, all three men constantly alert. Gerry Harlan, however, wore a left-hip holster due to the stiffness of his bandaged right arm.

Murray nodded toward a table occupied by four men. "The little guy's Lou Mallory and you've got to admit he's keeping pretty good company right now." The three with Mallory were County Judge Updegraff, Mayor Bill James and John Zollers, cashier of the Lake County Bank.

"He wasn't keeping very good company," Collier suggested, "when he hired Janford as his lawyer."

"You can't blame Mallory for that," Gerry argued. "It's a title suit and Janford *is* a good title lawyer. Mallory had no way of knowing he'd appoint a crooked caretaker at the mine."

Barry Holden came in, saw an empty chair at

the deputies' table and promptly took it. "I've got bad news for you boys." The reporter looked with a grin from Collier to Harlan. "Your best gals are running out on you. Ticket clerk at Sanderson's told me they just booked passage to Denver."

"On what coach?" Harlan asked.

"Tomorrow night's stage to Canon City. Seems Angela's pappy found out about Johnnie's call on the hill last night. They say he raised hell about it. So he's shipping her to where she can't keep company with bullet bait."

After a somber silence Murray asked, "What do you think of Lou Mallory, Barry?"

"I know one thing for sure," the reporter said. "He won't steal. Last month a man lost a wallet with four thousand dollars in it. Mallory found it and right away he put an ad in the *Chronicle*. The owner turned up and reclaimed his money."

"And Lou's been hard up for cash," Harlan said.

"He backs up Janford's story," Barry assured them. "Just to make sure I went out to see him this morning. His wife let me in. She's as fine a woman as you'll run into anywhere. Ask Angela and Lola. They think a lot of Ella Mallory. She left me alone with Lou and I asked him about Janford. He said yes, he retained Janford to represent him in the mine litigation, paid him a five thousand dollar fee in eight weekly payments and authorized him to put Rusk on as caretaker. Just like Janford told Tucker."

After a waitress served them Murray asked, "Have you seen Burris today?" Burris was the county attorney.

"I just came from him," Barry said. "He got a wire from Frisco which says there's no record that Ada Culp made a divorce application there."

"She's only been there a month," Murray reminded them.

But Collier, remembering points brought up last night by Angela Rand, wasn't impressed.

In early afternoon he left the hotel with Harlan and Murray. The three walked down Harrison to the sheriff's office. A property clerk on duty there was new. "Tucker fired the old one," Harlan said.

"Why?" Murray asked.

"Found out the guy was spending more money than he earned. Where did he get it? Nobody knows. But there've been leaks here; and at lots of other county and city offices."

A spectacles case, Collier remembered, had disappeared. The discharged clerk, for a bribe, could have connived at it.

Hoofbeats drummed in the street and a bone-weary posse pulled up. Tucker and eight men, sweaty and haggard, dismounted from jaded horses. "Didn't even get a shot at 'em." The sheriff's tone was disgusted as he came stiffly in.

He slumped with a sigh into his swivel chair. "They led us to hell and gone through the hills," he said. "Then they circled to the head of California Gulch and rode down it toward town. Last good sign we saw was just below Iron Hill. It faded out on a slag heap at Grant's smelter. I figure they hit Leadville just before daybreak and scattered."

"You look beat, Sheriff." The new property clerk handed him a cup of coffee.

After a swallow or two Tucker cocked an eye at Harlan. "Any new devilment here, Gerry?"

Harlan grinned at Collier. "Get ready to duck, Johnnie. He'll find it out anyway so we might as well tell him now."

Tucker listened impassively to the news about Collier's truancy from room 278, and the gunfight with Rufe Kansas.

To Collier's surprise, the sheriff gave him no worse than a sadly rebuking stare. "It's water over the dam," he said. "And it leaves us with one less killer to watch out for. That Rufe Kansas was a mean one."

"If we pick off enough of them," the new property clerk said, "maybe the rest of 'em 'll dig out of here and leave Collier alone."

Monte Murray didn't think so. "Where there's big money there's always someone who'll hire out his gun for it." He told Tucker that Duggan had put him on as an extra bodyguard.

The sheriff promptly approved. "Duggan did just right. And if it's okay with him, I'll have you transferred to the county force, Monte, as long as you're needed to guard Collier." He looked up grimly at Collier. "Betcha the payoff man's sweatin' blood right now, account of you rememberin' Rufe Kansas."

"What do you want us to do now, Sheriff?"

"Stick together, the three of you. To make yourselves useful, check every livery barn and corral in the city for Gus Culp's horses. If they got in during the night they had to leave their mounts somewhere. But they'd split up, no two men going to the same barn or corral. Play it for what it's worth, Gerry. And take care of that sore arm. Goshomighty, I'm tired. Somebody pull off my boots."

The three deputies went out and began a round of the city's stock shelters. At each they asked what horses had been brought in during the night and early morning.

Many mounts had to be checked and generally the case was above suspicion. Other mounts had been left by drifters. At Gray's stable on lower Elm the hostler pointed out a roan pony. "The night man said it was dang near foundered when a guy left it here just before daylight. The guy was a stranger and according to the book, his name's Jones."

"Looks like a roan I saw at the Mallory mine barn," Harlan said.

Monte Murray called in a constable and put

him on guard. "If a man comes for that roan, hold him, Charley."

At each stable Harlan asked if a customer last night had limped. No barnman remembered a limper. Gus Culp, they concluded, had unsaddled at some private barn or shelter. Leadville, which had mushroomed to a population of forty thousand, would have hundreds of sheds and private corrals.

At a State Street stable Harlan recognized a sorrel which had been ridden by Janford to Iowa Gulch yesterday. "Mel rented it," the barnman said. "A little while ago he took out another one."

"To go where?"

"He didn't say."

Two stables later they arrived in time to see Flint Hammond ride out and turn east toward Fryer Hill. The mount was a handsome bay whose saddle had silver trimmings. Hammond, looming tall in the stirrups, rode it with grace and distinction.

Monte Murray's eyes followed enviously. "I'd sure like to own that horse. They tell me Flint paid a thousand dollars for him. Reckon he can afford it, the way he's rakin' in dough."

"It's the one he rides every day," the hostler said, "when he goes out to his *Morning Star* mine."

# Eighteen

But this afternoon Flint Hammond gave the *Morning Star* a wide berth. He avoided Fryer Hill with its clanks of machinery and its brown dust clouds rising from an endless procession of ore carts. He took the opposite side of Fryer Hill from Big Strayhorse Gulch and in time reached Breece Hill, where mines were fewer and production comparatively light.

In an unproductive corner of Breece Hill he stopped at a shut-down mine in which, according to the county records, he still owned a half interest. And according to those same records the other half was owned by the estate of Job Norcross.

The same records would show that the estate of Job Norcross had no interest at all in the *Morning Star,* now the mighty Strayhorse Gulch bonanza of Flint Hammond. But the records were false. If the fraud ever came to light, Flint Hammond would owe the estate of Job Norcross half of all the huge fortune which had come out of the *Morning Star* mine. Not only that, but he'd owe the state of Colorado his own neck.

As for the *Evening Star,* Hammond had no choice but to keep it shut down. It had never produced more than fair wages for a two-man team working it. Yet even that pittance, if earned again by the mine, would legally need to be shared with the estate of Norcross. Which Hammond would hardly miss. But if he should send even one dollar to that estate, its administrator in Missouri would ask why, since just before his death Norcross had sold his interest in that claim to a partner named Flint Hammond. Any suspicion to the contrary would lead to Hammond's exposure.

For the same reason he didn't dare sell his own half interest in the shut-down mine. For the buyer might later try to acquire the other half and if he communicated with the Norcross estate's administrator, it would again lead to Hammond's exposure.

"So I'm stuck with it," Hammond muttered as he sighted the place.

There was a rusty winch with two ore buckets hanging in the shaft; a shaft house and two sheds, one for tools and one for stock. Also a one-room cabin where Hammond and Job Norcross had bached while working the claim.

The place had a look of complete abandonment. There was no sign of intrusion, and in fact nothing here worth stealing. Flint Hammond put his big bay horse in the stock shed and went to the cabin. It had aspen-pole walls, a dirt floor and a sod roof. Hammond unlocked it and went inside, grimacing at the cobwebby squalor of it. It was hard to believe that he, a silver king second only to Haw Tabor, had less than a year ago been grubbing for a bare living here.

He opened the one window to air the place, then made a fire in the stove. There were two home-made stools. He brushed the dust from one of them and sat down, waiting nervously for Mel Janford.

For no longer did he dare meet Janford at his suite in the Clarendon. He'd warned the lawyer never again to be seen speaking to him in public. It had been bad enough after Janford had lost his temper and punched a reporter for twitting him about cash deposits in a bank. But since yesterday the risk had become immeasurably worse. Yesterday when Janford had been caught calling at the Iowa Gulch hide-out!

Hammond wondered how the lawyer had managed to squirm out of that one. What hold did he have on Louis Mallory? Clearly Mallory was lying for him. No one knew better than Flint Hammond that the seven hundred dollars a week had been paid not by Mallory but by Hammond himself.

Looking out he saw Janford approaching on a brown pony. Sight of the man brought to Hammond a rush of burning anger. There was a gun in his pocket and for a moment he was tempted. Why not shoot that shyster and drop him in the shaft? That way he'd be rid of him forever.

But there'd still be Culp. Culp who knew much less than Janford, but still enough to hang Flint Hammond. And Janford was full of tricks. It would be like him to leave an accusing record somewhere.

Sullenly Hammond watched the man put his pony in the shed and walk toward the shanty. He seemed different today. Usually he was cocky, confident, often impudently derisive. Now he looked worried, uneasily cautious. Had some new danger cropped up in town? Had a second shutter of memory opened in the mind of Wesley Warren? How long would it be before that cowboy knew he was Wesley Warren, and not John Collier?

The meeting here was to face and prepare for that emergency. Objective number one was still to have one of Culp's gunmen eliminate Collier before he knew he was Warren. But the risks were getting too tight to depend on one plan alone. An alternative must be decided on. What could they do to save their skins and loot if plan number one failed?

Janford came into the cabin, his face humorless. "We're in a squeeze, Flint," he announced, and sat down on the other stool to roll a cigaret.

"Did Mallory change his story?" Hammond hoped it was no worse than that. For he himself had never had any dealings with Mallory. And Mallory knew nothing of the *Morning Star* fraud. Until yesterday he would have sworn that Mallory was on the level.

The lawyer spoke impatiently. "You don't need to worry about Mallory. He won't let me down."

"Why? What's your hold on him?"

"He's got a wife in a sanitarium back in Pennsylvania. Never mind how I found out. The wife he's got here doesn't know it. If she did, she'd leave him in a minute."

"So *that's* how you made him hire you in the mine suit!"

"You're wrong, Flint. I didn't make him hire me. He retained me because I've got title experience and was willing to accept a small fee. Which, by the way, he hasn't paid yet."

"But he told Tucker he paid you five thousand . . ."

For the first time Janford smiled. It was a twisted smile and from the same lips he blew smoke rings from his cigaret. "Until three days ago he didn't even know I knew about the Pennsylvania invalid. But when Barry Holden jumped me about those weekly bank deposits I was in a corner. So I went to Mallory and said: 'If anyone asks you about my fee in the Iowa Gulch case, say it was five thousand dollars and you've already paid it in eight weekly payments.

Either that or I'll tell Ella she's not your legal wife.' "

"I see. You couldn't put a money squeeze on him, like you did on me, because he's broke. But you *could* make him lie for you."

The lawyer shrugged. "Why not? I had to cover myself, didn't I? But forget Mallory. We're in a real jam now, Flint."

Janford's grimness frightened Hammond. He felt sure he was about to be told that Wesley Warren had regained a second link of his lost memory. "Let's have it." Hammond sat stiffly on the cabin stool, braced for the worst.

"I never did tell you how I got the goods on you, Flint."

"What difference does it make now?" Hammond blurted impatiently.

"It's time for you to know," Janford insisted. "Early last spring when the big rush of filings was on, County Clerk Rand hired an extra copy clerk for a few weeks. Name was McClure and I happened to know he was in debt and on the make. I slipped him a hundred bucks and told him to let me know if he ran into anything shady down there. I wasn't thinking of you, Flint. There'd been a good deal of claim and town lot jumping, some of it covered by forgeries in the county records.

"McClure's job was to check the ledger copyings of Raymond Otis against the original deeds or patents, before returning them to the owners. In doing so McClure stumbled on what looked like the syllable 'Mor' covering an erasure. The deed was in your favor, signed by Job Norcross and notarized in Kansas City by a Walter Cummings. McClure was too stupid to smell a million-dollar fraud. But I wasn't. I found out that Norcross had died, so I wrote the Kansas City notary asking the name of the mine involved. He answered saying it was the *Evening Star.*"

Hammond recalled that Angela Rand, a few days ago, had proposed making a similar inquiry on a broad scale. To keep her from doing it they'd had to steal and burn a ledger.

"Go on," Hammond said savagely.

"McClure was laid off when the spring rush ended. The other day Rand took him on again to help out in the current rush to re-record titles in the new Ledger B. So I slipped him another hundred dollars and told him to keep his eyes and ears open."

"For what?"

Janford puffed his cigaret. "That Rand girl's a lot smarter than her old man. She's helping out down there and so's her friend the school-teacher. The two of them have been chummy with Warren and Harlan. So if any inside infor-mation's on foot, the two girls would know and talk about it. They did—and McClure caught just enough of it to tip me off."

Hammond listened, a shade paler and more alarmed every minute. "Tipped you off to what? Get along, damn you! What the devil did you find out?"

"That Ada's in Denver, instead of in Frisco. And that the two girls are leaving for Denver on tomorrow evening's Canon City stage. They'll look up Ada. No one knows why they're going. Not even Rand, or Harlan, or Wesley Warren. They're doing it on the hush and no one knows but you and me. McClure's too dumb to count."

"So what? Ada won't tell them anything."

"She won't need to. One look at her and they'll know I'm her brother. She's got my chin and mouth and eyes. Which'll prove I'm a liar and tie me in a hard knot with Culp."

Hammond licked his lip and tried to disparage it. "You, but not me," he said.

"You too. Ada doesn't give a hang about you, Flint. Or about Gus Culp. But I'm her blood brother. It's for my sake, not yours or Culp's, that she hasn't talked. Once I'm scuttled she'll have no desire or reason to cover up for anyone else."

A moment's thought convinced Hammond that it was true. Even if she tried to hold out, Ada lacked the intelligence to match wits with two smart girls like Angela Rand and Lola Loomis. They'd soon have the truth out of her after she could no longer deny that she'd been born Ada

Janford. It was because Janford was Culp's brother-in-law that he'd been able to arrange for the Culp gang's return from Arizona to put teeth in his bite on Flint Hammond.

"I suppose you want me to send Buckshot Joe Wofford to Denver," Hammond said in a resigned voice, "to make sure Ada never talks."

The suggestion angered Janford. "What kind of a louse do you think I am? Don't forget Ada's my sister. If anything happens to her I'll see you hanged—even if they string me up on the same gibbet."

It was the first time Hammond had ever known Janford to stick at anything. "It's either that or we run, Janford. And I'm not ready to run yet. I'd need at least thirty or forty days."

The lawyer leaned forward with the old slyness back in his eyes. "There's a way you could buy thirty or forty days. That's why I came here to see you."

"Yes? Let's hear it."

The lawyer rolled another cigaret while Hammond waited with raw, edgy nerves. Ever since his near exposure by Bryson, Flint Hammond had been making secret preparations which even Janford didn't know about. He'd hoped there'd be no need to use them; but in case Culp's men failed to pick off Warren and the *Morning Star* fraud came to light, the last resort must be flight to Mexico or South America.

Hammond had already rented a safety box at each of the four Leadville banks. The four boxes were already bulging with currency and foreign bonds. Through an eastern broker he was buying heavily of French and Austrian securities, all negotiable. The *Morning Star* was netting him four thousand dollars a day and from now on it must all be stored away in ready cash or bonds. A forged passport could be purchased. Once he'd crossed the equator with his fortune, Ada's talk could do him no harm. Neither could Wesley Warren's.

"Come, Janford. How do I get it? The forty days of time?"

"Gus Culp and his men," the lawyer reminded him, "are stage robbers by trade. They did it in Arizona and they used to do it here. If I slip them a cash bonus, they'll be glad to hold up tomorrow night's Canon City coach. Besides the bonus, they'd get whatever they can take off the passengers."

"What good would that do us?"

"The stage gets to Buena Vista about midnight. That's where Cottonwood Creek empties into the Arkansas River. Along with his loot, Culp can take two hostages and make off with them; just to make sure there's no pursuit, he'll say. He fords the Arkansas and sends all but two men ahead to leave sign on Trout Creek Pass. It'll look like one of his prisoners kicked off a shoe there. The second shoe can be dropped on the trail through South Park. It'll make everyone think the hostages were taken east to the Platte. Actually two men take the hostages in the opposite direction, west up Cottonwood Creek toward the Continental Divide."

The hostages, Hammond assumed, would be Angela Rand and Lola Loomis. "It won't work, Janford. If those girls get hurt we'd be followed to the South Pole."

"They'll be too well chaperoned to get hurt. By Lippo and his wife Marta."

Of course! The hunting lodge in a mountain wilderness which Hammond had leased under an assumed name, preparing it as the jumping-off place for his own flight. Lippo and Marta were already installed, well supplied with food and comforts. It hadn't occurred to Hammond that he might need to hold hostages there. The place was only nine miles above the stage road at Buena Vista, up the south fork of Cottonwood Creek.

Marta was a woman with strong arms and a gentle Italian heart. She'd be disposed to shield two young girls in her charge from any rough treatment.

Hammond got up and paced the shanty's dirt floor. "What would it get us, Janford?"

"Forty days," the lawyer said.

"But Warren's likely to remember things before that!"

"It won't hurt us if he keeps his mouth shut. Which is the only way he can get his girl back. And Gerry Harlan's. We promise to release them in forty days. I'll find a way to let him know what the deal is."

"You'll leave my name out of it?"

*"Yes,"* Janford promised. "And mine too. There'll be just six people at the lodge. Lippo, Marta and the prisoners; the two men who take them there will stay as guards."

Hammond continued to pace like a caged coyote, torn between two terrors. The terror of being caught at once, through exposure by Ada in Denver, and the terror of living through the next forty days with a capital guilt hanging over him. The murder of Bryson alone would be enough to convict him. He could trust Lippo and Marta; beyond them he could trust no one, least of all Mel Janford.

"I've got to think it over, Janford."

Some of his old cynical brassiness returned to Janford. "Think fast, Flint. The dice are yours and it's a million-dollar throw. But make up your mind in the next five minutes. Culp and his men'll need all night and tomorrow to ride down there and get ready."

The lawyer twisted another cigaret, lighted it, blew coolly impertinent rings toward Hammond. "By the time I finish this smoke, say yes or no."

# Nineteen

The cowboy who knew himself only as John Collier awakened in room 278 with early morning sunlight at his window. Gerry was already up, scrubbing his face at the basin. The connecting door to 276 stood open and Collier could see Monte Murray pulling on his boots.

The night had been relatively quiet, all three men sleeping soundly after an afternoon and evening of combing the city for outlaw horses.

Because they'd accomplished nothing, a glumness settled on Collier as he began dressing. Angela would be leaving for Denver tonight. If her father had his way about it she'd go without seeing him again.

There was a knock on the door and Gerry Harlan, hand on gun, opened it cautiously. A hotel boy was there with a note. "It just came over from Lem Gray's barn," the boy said.

The name alerted Harlan as he closed the door. "Gray's," he said, "is the livery barn where we saw that outlaw roan."

Murray came in from the other room. "I posted a constable there," he reminded them, "in case someone called for the roan. Did he grab the guy?"

Gerry read the note, then swore under his breath.

"He was clipped on the jaw right after midnight. So was the night hostler. When they came to, the roan and its saddle were gone."

"Did they see who hit 'em?"

"No, blast it! It was done in the dark from behind. Let's get down there and have a look."

In the lobby they dispatched a porter to bring their mounts from the county corral. By seven o'clock they'd had breakfast and were riding to Gray's stable. The liveryman met them with a dour face. "There were five of 'em," he said.

"The note claims your night man didn't see them."

"He didn't. But Jennie Tolliver did." Gray pointed to a house across the street. "She happened to wake up and look out of her front window right after midnight."

The deputies crossed over to see Jennie Tolliver. "I looked out and saw four saddled horses," she told them. "They were tied in front of the livery barn. Nobody was in sight. Then five men came out of the barn. One of them was leading a saddled roan and another walked with a limp. They allfive mounted and rode off."

"In which direction?"

"That way." The woman pointed west down the dust of Elm Street.

The hoof-churned dust would show no tracks. "It was Culp and four of his heelers," Harlan said. "Tucker'll give us hell for this."

But the sheriff didn't. At the county jail he took

part of the blame himself. "Your report last night tipped me about that roan, Gerry. I should have sent a man there to help the constable keep an eye on it. But all my deputies were dead tired after that ride night before last."

Harlan, Collier and Murray rode the outlying streets, trying to find someone who'd seen the five outlaws leave town. The few responses were inexact and contradictory. "They went that way," a man said, pointing west toward the Sawatch Range. "They went that way," another said, pointing north toward Tennessee Pass.

Leadville boiled with rumors and by mid-afternoon the *Chronicle* had an extra on the street. The headlines said: CRISIS IN CULP CASE; QUINTET OF KILLERS ESCAPE; COW-BOY COLLIER UNDER DOUBLE GUARD; WILL HE LIVE TO REMEMBER?

Every angle of the mystery was played to the limit. "The *Chronicle* can hardly doubt," the lead editorial said, "but that some huge price has been offered for the snuffing out of Collier's life—provided it happens before he remembers who he is and why he is here. Nothing less could induce the Culp killers to take such bold risks. Their assignment has a deadline and they're out to beat it. So far their intended victim has remembered only one thing—the face of Rufe Kansas. Any day, any hour, any minute, he may remember something else."

All through the afternoon Collier looked hopefully for Angela Rand. But neither she nor Lola appeared at the Clarendon. "Her old man's got her under wraps," Monte Murray said. "But if I was you boys, I'd slick up a little. At six those gals of yours'll be boardin' a stagecoach; and there's no law against your seein' 'em off."

At six, in their best shirts and freshly shaved, Collier and Harlan stood on the walk in front of the Barlow and Sanderson station. Monte Murray hovered nearby, watching the street for possible snipers. The night coach for Canon City was loading its twelve passengers, three to each of its four seats. Friends crowded the sidewalk to see them off. It was one of the shiny new coaches recently shipped here from Concord, New Hampshire, where the finest stages in the world were made. Six matched bays stood in the traces, with a driver and a guard perched on the forward boot.

Angela and Lola were the last passengers to arrive. Milton Rand brought them in a hack, coolly ignoring John Collier as he handed them aboard. A station man stowed their baggage on the stage.

Angela had a window seat on the rear row. The window was open and she waved from it. "Good-bye, Johnnie."

Collier and Harlan pushed through the crowd and stood hats in hand at the window. Lola

Loomis sat just beyond Angela and Gerry Harlan called to her, "When'll you be back?"

"In time for school," Lola told him.

"And you, Angela?" Collier asked.

"I'm not sure, Johnnie. Dad says I must . . ."

"She'll stay there till it's safe to come back, young man." Milton Rand spoke at Collier's elbow, his tone crisp and uncompromising.

Lola leaned across Angela to speak through the window. "Write us, Gerry. We'll be staying at the Broadwell on Larimer Street."

"We sure will," Gerry promised.

"Have a good time," Collier said, "and don't get held up on the way."

Angela laughed. "No danger of that. Dad says this coach doesn't carry anything but passengers and mail."

"That's right," Harlan confirmed. He knew that express and bullion shipments went out on the shorter South Park Line over Mosquito Pass. "That's a right pretty hat you've got on, Lola."

"Yours too, Angela," John Collier said. Angela wore a dove-colored travel bonnet tied under her chin with ribbons. The older girl's hat was a wide-brimmed straw sailor covered by a dust veil and with a silver hatpin impaling it to her hair.

"But we're going to buy new ones," Angela said happily, "the minute we get to Denver."

Then with a lurch the coach was off. Angela

waved again and called out something which Collier lost amid the shouts and godspeeds of the crowd.

The sun had dipped behind the Sawatch snow-caps by the time the stage cleared town and took the dusty, deep-rutted road down the north rim of California Gulch. Passengers chattered for a while, then gradually grew silent. A miner's wife on the back seat with Lola and Angela unwrapped a pasteboard box and offered to share her fried-chicken supper.

"Thank you; but we've had supper," Lola said.

Black smoke ahead was the Malta smelter and a stop was made at the station there. But only to take on another mail pouch. "We're full up," the driver told people who wanted to get on. He cracked his whip and they were off down the east bank of the Arkansas River.

An hour later there was a stop to change horses and by then it was almost dark. Soon after that the stage crossed a wooden bridge to the west bank of the river. Looking from her west window Angela could see the skyline only as a dark wall of domes and peaks with the bulge of Mount Massive looming highest of all. Stars arched like tiny lamps across the ceiling of the night.

"You're sure you didn't tell anyone, Lola?"

"Not a soul," Lola said.

"Not even Gerry?"

"Him least of all. He would have told Johnnie Collier."

And Collier, Angela knew, was just as anxious to keep her out of risks as Milton Rand himself. "Imagine their surprise, Lola, when they hear how we've wormed the truth out of Ada and turned it over to the Denver police!"

Shortly before ten o'clock they crossed the county line and a little beyond it stopped at the Granite change station. Again the stage took on a sack of mail and fresh horses. Granite was the county seat of Chaffee County but soon the seat would be moved eighteen miles southeast to Buena Vista. The sheriff's office had already been moved there because it was closer to the county's center.

"Giddap!" The driver snapped his whip and they were off again. As the night grew colder Angela closed her window.

After they forded Clear Creek she fell asleep. Lola put an arm around her, drawing the younger girl's head to her shoulder. Her hatbrim was in the way, so Lola removed the veil and silver hatpin, laying the hat in her lap. On the other side of her the miner's wife slept audibly.

Presently Lola herself dozed and when she awoke it was midnight. Voices from a station platform told her that they were changing horses at Buena Vista.

The lurch of starting awakened Angela. "Are we on time?" she asked.

A traveling man on the seat ahead looked back at her. "Right on the dot, miss. They say we'll make Salida for breakfast. The Royal Gorge begins there. Always did want to see that gorge. Comin' in I took the Fremont Pass route from Georgetown."

They forded Cottonwood Creek, the coach wheels crunching across riffle-covered gravel. Then on down the west bank of the Arkansas, most of the passengers now sleeping.

Less than two miles out of Buena Vista they rounded a sharp curve and there was a rasp of brakes. The suddenness of the stop threw Angela forward and as she righted herself she heard voices from the road.

Looking out on the river side of the road she saw men with rifles. Two were aiming at the driver and his guard. Others were covering the coach windows. A gruff voice said: "Nobody'll be hurt unless he gets funny. Everybody pile out and line up."

There was a clatter as the driver and the guard tossed down their guns. An outburst of alarm filled the coach. Presently it was clear that six outlaws had stopped the stage by felling a sapling across the road.

"Get out and line up," the leader repeated. "We don't figger to hurt anybody if we can help it."

A woman near the front gave a half-smothered

scream; after that the order was obeyed with reasonable meekness. Except for two grizzled prospectors the male passengers were commercial men and probably unarmed. One by one they got out of the coach and stood in line by the road.

Angela and Lola were the last out. "Right over here, ladies. If any of you gents has got a gun he'd better not try to use it. All we want is your wallets and the registered mail. Buck, gather up whatever they've got on them. Monk, take a look and see if they left anything inside."

All the outlaws were masked. The one who gave the orders had a slight limp and Angela concluded he was Gus Culp. Only two days ago Sheriff Tucker had been chasing him through the hills above Leadville.

One outlaw went down the line to collect pocket money and watches. But to Angela's surprise he passed up her own purse and a ruby ring on her finger. The man called Monk reappeared from the coach with a collection of valuables he'd found under the seats.

He handed a black sailor hat to Lola Loomis. "Is this yours, lady?"

Lola gave a stare of confusion, then took the hat and put it on. Another outlaw opened the baggage carrier and tossed baggage out on the ground. "Everybody claim his own stuff," the lame man ordered.

Why, Angela wondered, did they want to

identify the baggage? She pointed out her own and so did Lola.

"Take it away," the lame man said. One of the outlaws picked up Lola's telescope and a Gladstone grip belonging to Angela. He disappeared into riverbank cottonwoods with them. The rest of the baggage was ignored.

"This is as fur as you gals go," the man called Monk announced. He took a firm hold on Lola's arm and another man took Angela's. "You ain't gonna be hurt none," he promised. "Just a little hossback ride, that's all."

The coach guard yelled: "Leave those girls alone!" He lunged forward to grapple with Monk but the lame man clubbed him down with a rifle barrel.

Lola's scream was too paralyzed with shock to carry far. Angela managed a better one before a grain sack was dropped over her head. She felt herself being dragged toward the riverbank grove. The man dragging her said: "Soon as we make a getaway you'll be turned loose. Both of you."

Angela heard the lame man giving final orders to the passengers. "We'll just cut a few trace tugs to delay you a little. All we want's a four-hour start. Soon as we get it we'll turn 'em loose. Pick up the guns, Buck, and let's ride."

In the cottonwood grove Angela felt herself being hoisted astride a saddle. It bunched her skirts awkwardly about her legs. One of her wrists was tied to the saddle horn and she sensed that the same treatment was being given Lola. The sack over her head kept her from seeing anything. "Don't make a fuss, lady," a man said. "Start yellin' and I'll have to stuff a rag in your mouth."

"Fetch along their baggage, Monk, and let's fan outa here."

Her mount moved forward and Angela knew it was being led. But almost at once a rush of water at her stirrups told her they were fording the Arkansas. It came ice cold over her ankles, drenching her to the knees. She heard a moan of distress from Lola and by the splashing sounds she knew they were riding single file.

The horses stumbled and skidded on the slippery stones of the river's bed. A man leading Angela's mount turned to curse it on. Then they were splashing out on the east bank and by the swish of underbrush and the smell of damp tree bark Angela knew they were in another cottonwood grove.

A brief halt was made and one of the outlaws dismounted. "You need some dry shoes, miss." To Angela's further befuddlement he took off her shoes and replaced them with what felt like doeskin moccasins.

"Get going," the lame man said. And it was the last time Angela ever heard his voice.

She could tell by the hoof sounds that the outlaws were splitting into two parties. Her own mount was led through trees up the riverbank. Lola's terrified, "Where are you taking us?" came from directly behind Angela. But other hoof sounds faded out in a direction at right angles to the river.

From here on the only voices Angela heard were those of Monk and Buck. "Not fur, miss." It was Buck's answer to Lola's last question.

Twice Monk repeated his assurance. "You ain't gonna be hurt none. Just don't make any fuss."

Underbrush kept swishing at Angela's legs with the rushing river always at her left. Suddenly they began fording it again. And again the cold current came to the hem of Angela's bunched skirt. Why, she wondered, were they recrossing the river?

When the crossing was completed they were still in water, but in shallower and less turbulent riffles. For a long time they continued to splash up those riffles without wading out of them. Angela guessed that the second fording of the Arkansas had been made opposite the mouth of a tributary stream coming in from the west. It would have to be Cottonwood Creek, which joined the river near Buena Vista.

"Why did you take my shoes?" Angela asked forlornly. The second fording had soaked the moccasins she'd been given in exchange.

"To prove we've got you," Monk said.

What for? she wondered. Would they demand a

ransom payment? "Can you see anything, Lola?"

"How can I," Lola said wretchedly, "with this bag over my head?"

At last the file of horses waded out of the creek and took a trail up its left bank. The sack had air holes in it and Angela felt no shortness of breath. "Did they take your shoes too, Lola?"

"No," Lola said. And for a while after that there was no sound except the clop of hooves on gravel. Cold and numb, Angela tried desperately to marshal her wits and keep a mental log of this travel. There was no way to measure time. But the sound of riffles at her right told her they were on an upstream trail.

Then a new and tangier smell meant that pine timber was beginning to replace creekbank willows and cottonwoods. That double fording of the big river, she reasoned, had been a trick to hide the true trail. Some of the outlaws could be making a false one in another direction.

Lola asked dismally, "Are you all right, Angela?"

"All except my feet," Angela said. "I think they're frozen."

The voice of Buck said: "Soon you'll be warm. A woman will take care of you."

He sounded sincere. What woman? Angela wondered. Could she be Ada? Had Ada made up with Culp and been installed as mistress of some mountain hide-out?

The ascent steepened and creek sounds were

now from cascades instead of from riffles. Angela's knees scraped pine bark and she sensed that they were in a thickly grown forest. It seemed hours since she'd been imprisoned in this saddle. But no hint of daylight came through the holes of her head bag. How far had they ridden? Three hours up a mountain trail would be only about nine miles.

Progressively the trail got steeper, the air colder, the pine trees thicker. Shivering, Angela took her feet from the stirrups and swung her legs to get the stiffness out of them. She heard a plaintive plea from Lola: "I can't stand this any longer; please let me get off and walk."

Monk answered quietly: "We'll be there in a minute. I see a lantern."

A halt was called and Angela's wrist was released from the saddle horn. "Get down," Buck said, and she slid awkwardly to the ground.

Voices came from nearby and one of them was a woman's. Through the air holes of her sack Angela glimpsed the lambency of a lantern. A woman's hand touched her arm and a woman's voice said gently: "Your rooms are ready, *signorinas.* Come."

"Where's Lola?"

"Here I am." Lola's cold hand groped for her own and someone led them both up porch steps. They passed through a doorway and immediately there was warmth.

"I have made a fire for you," the woman guide said.

But the fire wasn't in this room for they were led across it and along a hallway beyond. This clearly was no mere mountain cabin but a house of generous proportions. At the end of the hall they were guided up a staircase and through a doorway at the top. Angela heard the crackle of a fire. The woman said: "Put their baggage down, Buck, and leave us."

There were the sounds of Buck's departure. Then the sack was taken from Angela's head. She stood staring about her: at a bedraggled Lola; at the appointments of a richly furnished apartment; and at a woman of enormous girth who might be either Spanish or Italian. Her soft black eyes had kindness in them.

"Are you Ada?" Angela asked incredulously.

"I am Marta," the woman said. "My duty is to make you comfortable. I will see that no harm comes to you here." She motioned toward the baggage. "You will first put on dry clothes. The bedroom is in there." She pointed to an inner door. "If you desire hot water, you have only to ring a bell."

Angela took off her bonnet and Lola her rudely crushed straw hat.

"When you are dry and warm," the woman said, "I will bring you a pot of tea." She left the apartment and closed the door behind her. Angela heard a bolt click as she locked them in.

# Twenty

The sun was an hour high when three grim young men, each leading a remount, loped past the Malta smelter. Collier and Harlan rode abreast, Monte Murray a few lengths behind. Not a word had been spoken since they'd spurred out of Leadville on the stage road for Buena Vista.

Six miles beyond Malta they drew up at a relay station. But only to change saddles to the remounts. "Anything new on the wire?" Harlan asked. The telegraph wire which followed the Canon City stage line was cut in at many of the relay stations.

"Nothin' since I heard that message go through at two a.m.," the station man said. "You boys joinin' the posse?"

Collier and Harlan were too preoccupied to answer; but Murray wasn't. "You couldn't keep 'em out of it with a shotgun; not with their best girls gettin' packed off by the Culpers."

They rode impatiently on. Tucker had aroused them before daybreak, showing them a telegram from Chaffee County. "It ain't in my jurisdiction, boys. Sheriff Potter'll handle it."

But he'd been unable to keep Collier and Harlan

from joining the manhunt. And because Murray's assignment was to stick with John Collier, he too had saddled up for Buena Vista.

They crossed a bridge over the river and turned down its west bank. "All I ask," Gerry said savagely, "is to get that guy in my sights." The others knew he meant Gus Culp.

"I figure he was lying," Collier said, "when he claimed he was taking them along just to get a four-hour start. The four hours were up at daybreak and if he turned them loose, they'd 've been picked up by someone on the road."

"Maybe they have," Murray said. "Maybe we'll get word of it at Granite."

But the station master at Granite had no further word of the hunt. Again the three riders shifted saddles and pressed on. To the west of them the Continental Divide made a curtain of rocky peaks, timber sloping steeply down from the snow lines. It was thirty-five miles from Leadville to Buena Vista and hard-riding horsemen, with remounts, could make it in five hours.

At exactly noon they spurred into Buena Vista and drew up at Sheriff Potter's Office. Potter's chief deputy, Bud Ingalls, came out with what looked like a woman's shoe.

He knew Harlan and guessed his errand. "They went east over Trout Creek Pass, Gerry, and lit out across South Park. Potter's hard after 'em. He sent me back with this shoe."

At once Collier knew it was Angela's. "Where did you find it?"

"Right smack in the middle of the road where the stage trail to Fair Play crosses Trout Creek Pass. Purty smart of that gal, I say. She must've kicked it off in the dark, so we'd know which way they took her."

Trout Creek Pass was only fourteen miles east of the holdup spot. Heading that way with two hostages, the outlaws would cross it about an hour before daybreak.

"We'll be right after 'em," Harlan said, "soon as we grain our broncs."

While the horses were being grained they sent a telegram to Tucker telling where the shoe had been found. Then the three deputies ate hurriedly and set out to join Potter's posse.

After fording the Arkansas they followed a stage trail which branched easterly from the Canon City road in the direction of South Park. "It forks a few miles the other side of the pass," Harlan told Collier. "One fork goes northeast to Fair Play; the other heads due east to hit Eleven Mile Canyon of the Platte."

A little short of the pass they met a stagecoach headed west. The driver pulled up. "You boys gonna join up with Potter?"

"That's right."

"When you get to the split, take the right-hand fork. They took the gals that way."

"How do you know?"

The driver held up a woman's shoe, the mate to one Bud Ingalls had shown them. "She kicked off the other one too. Potter said for me to take it to town so folks'll know he's on the right track." He whipped his horses and the coach rolled on.

In late afternoon the three Leadville men crossed Trout Creek Pass. From there they rode down into an open park some twenty miles in any dimension. It was floored with tall grass and surrounded by pine-clad mountains. The South Fork of the Platte wound through it in innumerable gooseneck curves.

At the near edge of the park the road split and they took the right-hand fork. "I reckon it was about here Angela kicked off her other shoe," Murray said. "Wonder what she dropped next."

Collier pondered it. "She could drop things in the dark, Monte, without them seeing her. But not in daylight."

"Dark'll be catching *us,*" Harlan worried, "before *we* can catch up with Potter."

Collier reined to a halt. "Hold on, fellas; that gives me an idea."

"We could use an idea, Johnnie. What's on your mind?"

"Daylight and dark," Collier said. "Look. We leave Buena Vista a little after noon and dark catches us about here. Culp's gang leaves the holdup a little after midnight and daybreak

225

catches them about here. In daylight they can't stay on a traveled road with two women prisoners."

"Right, Johnnie. Not in an open park like this."

"So as soon as light came they'd need to get under cover." Collier waved his hand toward the broad sweep of grass, bare of trees.

But on the hillsides sloping down to it were dense banks of pine and aspen. Collier pointed. "Nearest cover from here is that neck of timber to the south. Lowest tip of it's not over three miles away."

"It'd be the quickest way they could get out of sight," Gerry agreed. "Let's look for grass sign."

They rode on and a half mile farther could see a dim line where stirrup-high grass had been ridden through by a file of mounted men. It pointed toward the nearest mountainside timber. "Let's hope Potter saw it and went that way too," Harlan said. "Let's go."

They left the road and moved south, following dim disturbance sign through high grass.

"Look! Someone's coming." John Collier pointed toward a horseman who was emerging from hillside trees. The man came at a lope straight their way.

As he drew nearer Harlan recognized him. "It's Podge Kelly, one of Potter's deputies."

Kelly met them and drew up. "Hi, Harlan. Look what we found." He held up a government mail sack which had been slit open. "We picked it up in the woods about four mile south of here."

According to the stage driver's report, a sack of registered mail had been taken by the holdup men. When they'd felt safe from pursuit they'd looted it and thrown away the bag.

"Potter wants it reported by telegraph," Kelly said, "so everybody'll know they're headin' south toward the Badger Crik country."

"Where'll we find Potter? We want to join up."

The Chaffee County deputy twisted in his saddle to point in the direction from which he'd come. "You'll find camp ashes just inside those trees. Follow the sign from there."

Podge Kelly loped on to make his report at Buena Vista, while the three Leadville men rode toward the tree line. Somewhere beyond it they'd overtake a posse and with it continue on the trail of Gus Culp.

"Wait till I get that guy in my sights!" Harlan muttered fiercely.

"He oughta be staked out on an ant hill," Murray said, "makin' off with womenfolks like that!"

But John Collier was beginning to have doubts. Some of the outlaws had clearly gone this way. But had all of them? Had Angela really kicked off her shoes in the dark? Or had they been dropped on purpose by Culp?

# Twenty-one

Leadville sizzled with reports and rumors, some true, some false. As he stood at the Clarendon bar, Flint Hammond heard a medley of them. Nothing else held the ear of Leadville these days; bonanzas could boom or collapse, but nothing could distract attention from a sensational manhunt in the hills below South Park. Deputies from four counties had joined it. Every hour the telegraph wires brought the latest news of it.

The outlaws were at bay, one report said, in a cabin on Badger Creek. A girl's scream had been heard from the cabin and so the besieging posse was afraid to shoot into it. Another rumor had it that the hostages had been released and had found refuge, half dead from shock and exposure, at a sheepherder's camp. Two of Angela Rand's shoes and a gutted mail sack had been picked up along the route of flight.

To these and other rumors Flint Hammond listened with jumping nerves. He knew which were true and which weren't. Culp was smart; he was like a fox in the woods outwitting the hounds.

"I'd hate to be Culp," a man at the bar said, "if they ever ketch up with him. They'll cut him into pound chunks and feed him to the magpies."

"Two of 'em will, I betcha," another man said. "Harlan and young Collier. They're fit to be tied, I betcha."

Hammond finished his drink and went up to his second-floor suite. The keyring he took from his pocket had seven keys on it. He used the first of them to unlock the hall door—the one with the silver horseshoe over it. Once inside, he used the second key to enter his office beyond the sitting room; and the third to open a safe there.

In the safe Flint Hammond stored an envelope which had come to him in today's registered mail from a broker in New York. The envelope held thirty thousand dollars' worth of Austrian bonds, exchangeable for cash in any part of the world. He put them with many other such bonds already in the safe.

After relocking the safe Hammond looked critically at the four other keys on his ring. They would open as many private safety boxes at the four Leadville banks. Each box held cash in large bills. With the cash and the bonds, should worse come to the worst, he could quickly disappear. Every day he remained here in command of the *Morning Star* mine would serve to increase that portable fortune by another four thousand dollars.

So far not an eyebrow had been raised. In the Leadville district there were seventeen smelters and Hammond had made a practice of dividing the *Morning Star*'s ore output among them. The smelters refined and marketed his production and each sent him a weekly check. It kept any one check from being too conspicuously large when he cashed it or mailed it to an eastern broker with an order to buy bonds.

But now a new hazard occurred to Hammond. Banks were open only six hours a day and on Sundays not at all. Suppose a telegram of exposure came during a night or a weekend! News that Culp's hostages had been found at a mountain lodge in the custody of Hammond's ex-servant Lippo! Or suppose that Wesley Warren should suddenly remember that he was the nephew of a man who'd once owned a half interest in the *Morning Star!*

In either case Hammond would need to run fast and far with whatever he could lay hands on at the moment. If at night it would mean abandoning a cash fortune at the banks.

The risk brought Hammond to a decision. He took a leather satchel in which he'd often carried valuables to or from a bank, locked all doors of his suite and left the hotel. His banks were the First National, the Miners' Exchange, the Lake County Bank and the Bank of Leadville.

He went first to the First National on Harrison Avenue.

Mr. Raynolds, the president, waved a genial hand as Hammond passed on his way to the safety-box vault. "Putting it in or taking it out, Flint?"

Hammond was taking it out, but he didn't say so. Shortly he was back in his hotel suite, storing ninety thousand dollars in his office safe.

Later he made similar transfers from the three other banks.

At dinner that evening in the Clarendon dining room he watched alertly for Mel Janford, who habitually dined there. But never with Flint Hammond. Janford was under a cloud and Hammond wasn't. At least there were some who suspected Janford of collusion with the Culp gang. Not for anything would Hammond let himself be seen with Janford.

Yet in an emergency the lawyer might need to be consulted. Mel Janford had a gift for finding out things. He had ears everywhere and a paid spy at the sheriff's office. If a revealing telegram came from the man-hunters, Janford would promptly know about it.

In such a case he'd need to warn Hammond or at least arrange a meeting. The only place where they could meet without being seen was where they'd met before—at the *Evening Star* shanty on Breece Hill.

Tonight, should the signal be flashed, Hammond would have to saddle up and ride there at once.

All about him he heard a hum of talk and much of it concerned two Leadville girls who'd been carried away from a stagecoach holdup. Were they still alive? Were they ransom pawns? Did it have anything to do with the Bryson-Collier mystery?

County Clerk Milton Rand, haggard from sleepless nights, came in to look desperately from table to table, then went out again. No doubt he was hunting for Sheriff Tucker to get the latest word from the chase.

At last Mel Janford came in and took his usual table. Hammond watched covertly for a signal. Habitually the lawyer ordered claret wine with his dinner. But if he should order white wine it would be a prearranged message to Flint Hammond. "Ride out to the *Evening Star* and I'll meet you there."

Tonight the wine served to Janford was red and Hammond relaxed. Thus far, at least, all was well.

There were more sleepless nights and many more days of dread—not only for Milton Rand and the relatives of Lola Loomis but for most of the law-abiding people of Leadville. Suspense tightened and indignation grew feverish. Rawboned miners who didn't know either Angela or Lola talked of little else, as August ended and September began tinting the mountainside aspens with gold. At a dozen bars lynch parties were organized, to be ready with ropes when Culp was caught and brought to town.

But the outlaw wasn't caught, nor were any of his men. Their sign, according to reports from the manhunt, had been blotted out by the tracks of range horses feeding in a Fremont County meadow. Tracks of other horsemen, picked up and followed, had led only to the camps of honest men.

Potter himself gave up, finally, and took his crew back to Buena Vista. One by one others quit the chase until only three were left: the three from Lake County, Collier, Murray and Harlan.

And from them, to the anxious waiting in Leadville, came only silence. Each passing day another seventy tons of ore were hauled from the *Morning Star* mine to the Leadville smelters; each day netting another four thousand dollars for Flint Hammond and each week another seven hundred for Mel Janford.

Each evening at dinner Hammond watched sharply for a sign from Janford, always hoping there'd never be one, or need for one. Days shortened as September grew older, colder. And still no signal from Mel Janford.

No news was good news, Hammond concluded hopefully. If Wesley Warren had regained any part of his memory he'd be back in Leadville by now, to point an accusing finger.

Hammond met City Marshal Duggan on Harrison Avenue. "Tucker hasn't given up yet, has he, Duggan?"

Duggan grimaced. "Tucker hasn't. But I have. My guess is Culp got scared off; too much heat on; so likely he dropped 'em in some mine shaft and lit out for Arizona." The marshal lowered his voice. "But don't tell Milt Rand I said that. He's sick enough already."

It was mid-September when the last of the man-hunters quit beating the bush for Culp. They rode wearily into Leadville, put up their horses and came into the Clarendon so unkempt and bearded the desk clerk didn't at once recognize them. John Collier's eyes were bloodshot as he called for keys to rooms 276 and 278.

He went up with Harlan and Murray and found the rooms just as they'd left them. Monte Murray opened the connecting door and raised the windows. One look in a mirror made Harlan say, "We'd better get a bath and a shave or they won't let us in the dining room."

"We sure smell like sheepherders," Monte agreed.

They went back downstairs and into the hotel barbershop. "Hot water for three," Collier said.

He took a bath while Harlan shaved, and was shaved while Harlan bathed. Waiting his turn, Monte Murray had a drink at the bar.

It let Collier and Harlan finish first. "Come on up, Monte," Gerry said, "soon as you get through."

He and Collier went back up to room 278 whose door wasn't locked. There'd seemed no reason to lock it, since they'd only left for an hour at the barbershop.

But as Collier stepped inside he knew at once that someone had been here during that hour. The connecting door to 276, left open, was now closed. And on 278's table stood a pasteboard box about a foot and a half in any of its cubical dimensions. The box was sealed with tape.

A printed address on it said: COLLIER and HARLAN; CONFIDENTIAL.

Harlan used a knife to rip the top from the box. Bulky contents were wrapped in tissue paper on which lay a printed note:

Collier and Harlan:

The two hostages are safe and will be released October 4th on following conditions:

1. That you don't tell anyone about this warning.
2. That if Collier remembers anything, he keeps his mouth shut till Oct. 4th.
3. That you don't make trouble in any way.

Obey the above and hostages will show up unharmed on October 5th. Disobey and you'll never see them again.

There was no signature. But clearly the message was from Culp or from Culp's backer. Collier was certain that it hadn't been delivered by a hotel boy but had been slipped in furtively by someone from the outside.

Proof came when they removed the tissue paper and saw what lay beneath. A dove-colored traveling bonnet was there, the one Angela had worn on the stage. Pierced through it was a silver hatpin. And under the bonnet lay the black straw sailor worn by Lola Loomis.

After a hollow silence Gerry Harlan said slowly: "What do you think, Johnnie? Should we tell Tucker?"

John Collier read again the last line of the message—*You'll never see them again!* It was a lethal warning and the hats proved the message was no hoax. "We'll tell *nobody*," he decided. "Not even Monte."

After a moment of indecision Gerry agreed. "You're right, Johnnie. Whoever wrote this note means it. It's up to us and nobody else."

Collier read the note again, then burned it. "Hide the hats, Gerry, before Monte sees them."

# Twenty-two

From the curtained corner Gerry brought a duffel bag with which he'd arrived on first being assigned to guard John Collier. It had a change of clothing and an extra pair of boots. Gerry Harlan shook them out on the floor, then wedged the box

236

with the hats into the bag. After putting back the clothing and boots he tossed the duffel bag again behind the curtain. "Reckon that'll hide it, Johnnie."

"We'll be watched," Collier was sure, "by whoever brought the box in here; watched to see if we go running to the police."

Harlan nodded. "If we go to the Rand house they'll figure we're tipping off Milt Rand. I'd tell Tucker except there's always been a leak down there. No use telling Monte till we have to. When it's time for gunplay we can let him in on it."

The hats not only proved that Culp's men had the hostages confined at some hide-out, but that one of them had just arrived from there and was still in Leadville. It might be Culp himself. More than a week had gone by since the outlaw sign had faded out some sixty miles southeast of here.

"Don't forget, Johnnie," Gerry cautioned, "that their number one job's still to put a slug through you before you can recollect what's what. From now on they'll try harder than ever. That slug'll be laying for you every time we walk down the street."

They were walking down the street, an hour later, to check with Sheriff Tucker—Collier in the middle with his friends siding him.

"When I went into the hotel bar," Monte Murray said, "I was just in time to see a bet paid. The barkeeper handed five thousand dollars to Vic Werner. The month's up, Johnnie. You remember One-Card Connerly bet him you wouldn't stay alive that long."

At his office Sheriff Tucker listened to a report which made no mention of hats or a warning message.

"All we ask," Collier said, "is for you to let us keep on hunting the Culpers a while longer. We've a hunch some of them are back in town."

"While we're hunting *them*," Gerry added, "they'll be hunting Johnnie. So Monte and I want to stick right with him till showdown time."

"Name your poison," Tucker agreed. "The county'll pick up the check. It owes those guys a hanging. I'm not forgetting they killed a county deputy, Cal Barstow, not to mention Bryson and a flock of snipe shots at Collier."

"Thanks." The three deputies went out and back to the Clarendon.

At dinner they saw Melville Janford eating alone. Across the dining room Vic Werner was sharing a table with Flint Hammond. Barry Holden breezed in, saw the three gunslung deputies and joined them. "What about a scoop?" he coaxed.

"We don't know a thing," Collier said, "except that we're still looking for Culp."

"Sure, Johnnie; and you can bet he's still looking for *you*."

"If you see him, Barry, tell him where to find me."

John Collier could have been found that night, by Culp or anyone else, walking the streets of Leadville with Harlan and Murray. Sometimes on lighted streets, like Harrison, Chestnut or State; sometimes on dark streets like Poplar and Pine. "If they'd cut loose," Harlan said, "it'd give us something to shoot back at."

Or Collier could have been seen the next day inquiring at the livery barns. "One of Culp's men rides a roan," he told the liverymen. And Murray added: "From tracks we followed, one of the holdup horses has a flat shoe on the left front hoof."

Each barnman promised to watch out for such mounts.

Three days and three nights went by and no bullet came from a sniper. Nor was there a further message of warning. For hours on end the three deputies stood on a walk across from steps leading up to the law office of Melville Janford. But all clients who called there seemed to be reputable. From Barry Holden they learned that Janford had made no more large cash deposits at his bank.

The three fruitless days dragged by and still only Collier and Harlan knew about the hatbox message. "We're being played for suckers, Johnnie," Gerry said out of Murray's hearing. "They could have done away with the girls long ago and kept the hats to string us along with."

"Why would they string us along?"

"Maybe for time to finish some big clean-up. That's likely why they gave us a phony October deadline."

Collier couldn't deny the logic of it. "If we don't come up with something tomorrow," he said miserably, "I guess we'd better go tell Tucker and Mr. Rand. They've got a right to know."

It was in the middle of that fourth night that a sudden startling thought made John Collier sit bolt upright in bed. He threw off the covers, lighted the room and wakened Harlan.

"We missed something, Gerry."

"What?" Gerry blinked drowsily.

"A silver hatpin."

"No we didn't. It's stuck through Angela's hat."

"But her hat's a bonnet with strings to tie under the chin. It doesn't need a hatpin. The hatpin, you'll remember, belongs to that flat straw hat of Lola's."

Harlan got up, pulled on his pants and took the duffel bag from the curtained closet. In a minute they had the hatbox out and from it they took a hat and a bonnet. The wide-brimmed straw sailor, which needed a hatpin, didn't have one; but the bonnet did.

"It ought to be the other way, Gerry."

"I guess the Culpers got mixed up," Harlan said.

"Or maybe," Collier countered, "Angela heard

them planning to let us see the hats. So maybe she wrote a tip-off note and put it in her hat."

"It would fall out," Gerry argued, "when they packed it on a long horseback ride to town."

"Not if she used a hatpin," Collier said, "to make sure it didn't."

Harlan inverted the dove-colored bonnet and looked hopefully in it. He failed to see a message. "Guess again, Johnnie."

Collier took a closer look and saw that the bonnet was lined with silk. For a few inches along one side the lining seam showed threads which didn't match the machine threading around the rest of the circumference of the bonnet. "Maybe she ripped it a little way and then sewed it up again." In a taut excitement Collier tore away the entire lining.

"There it is, Gerry!"

Affixed securely by a silver hatpin to an inner wall of the bonnet was a square of paper with writing on it.

"Can't you fellas let a guy sleep?" The excited talk had awakened Monte Murray who now appeared in the doorway from room 276.

"Come on in, Monte," Harlan invited. "It's time you're in on this."

John Collier unpinned the note and read it aloud:

We're being held on the second floor of a large house in a pine forest. We can hear a creek but can't see it. On the way here we forded the river twice and then rode about three hours up a small stream. We're unhurt and have been treated well. Three men and one woman guard us. They've only let us see the woman. Her name is Marta and she weighs two hundred pounds. One man is called Buck and another Monk. The house is expensively furnished with

There was no more. "Maybe she heard someone coming and had to stop right there. Do you know of a big two-story house in the woods, Gerry?"

"I never saw it," Harlan said. "But a year ago there was talk of some rich New Yorker building a hunting lodge upmountain from Buena Vista."

"He died right after that," Monte remembered. "There was a squib in the *Chronicle* about it."

John Collier reached for his boots. "Then what are we waiting for? Let's saddle and ride."

In less than an hour they were riding fast out of Leadville. Again they took the Canon City stage road and again each man led a remount. "That lodge is up Cottonwood Creek," Murray said.

"Cottonwood's got two forks, Monte. Which one's it on?"

Murray didn't know. "But likely it's the south fork. The trail to Cottonwood Pass goes up the north fork. As I remember the paper said the rich

New Yorker picked a spot as far off the travel routes as he could get. First he was going to build on Chalk Creek. Then he found out that the trail to St. Elmo and Tincup Pass runs up Chalk. So he switched to the Cottonwood."

Alternately they walked and loped the horses. The first stage station was dark. But at the second, Granite, there was a breakfast light. Dawn was breaking over the Mosquito Range.

They pulled up at Granite for coffee and scrambled eggs. "You boys out after Culp again?" the station man asked.

"There's a rumor," Harlan evaded, "that he was seen at Salida so we thought we'd take a look down that way."

A few miles farther on a Leadville-bound stage-coach passed them. Its company would eat breakfast at Granite.

"Know anyone named Buck or Monk?" Collier asked as they rode on.

"Not Monk," Harlan said. "But Buck might be Buckshot Joe Wofford. He was with Culp at the Iowa Gulch mine."

The sun came brightly over the Mosquitoes and when it was an hour high the deputies crossed Three Elk Creek. Buena Vista lay less than half an hour ahead. But they'd decided not to confide in anyone there. If they did their mission would soon become public and a gossipy operator might relay it by wire to Leadville.

"For all we know Culp's got a man at Buena Vista," Gerry said. "He might beat us to the lodge and give a warning."

So they veered from the stage road and struck Cottonwood Creek two miles above its mouth. A wagon trail on its bank led westerly toward Cottonwood Pass. The deputies followed it to where the stream forked.

A good deal of public travel went up the north fork but only a dim trail went up the south. "I hear there's nothing up there," Murray said, "but a string of small lakes."

They rode up the south fork and with every mile the trail steepened. A dense forest of fir and pine gave no sound except from the cataracts of the creek. Collier recalled a line from Angela's note: "We can hear a creek but can't see it."

"Wildest country in Colorado's up this way," Murray said. "It's bear and elk country. There's three high glacier mountains right ahead of us but you can't see 'em for the trees. They call 'em Mounts Harvard, Princeton and Yale."

"We're clop-cloppin' too much," Harlan warned. "Lead my horse and let me scout ahead on foot."

The tall deputy walked ahead and the others kept five minutes back of him. Around three more twists of the trail they saw him reappear, his hand raised to stop them. "Grab your rifles, boys, and hide the horses." He pointed uphill.

"The lodge is only a shake that way. If it wasn't for the creek sounds they'd 've heard us comin'."

The six mounts were tied out of sight well off the trail and from there the three men moved alertly forward, rifles in hand. When the lodge came suddenly into view its size startled Collier. It was a two-story log building with verandas and a stone chimney, and looked more like a resort than a private hunting lodge. Back of it were sheds and a stable. "Golly!" Murray exclaimed. "Whoever put up that layout had money to burn."

"First let's scout the barn," Harlan said.

Keeping out of sight in the trees they circled to the barn's rear. A corral there had a team of carriage horses and a nearby shed sheltered a buckboard. Harlan took a look in the stable. "Four saddle horses," he reported. "One of 'em's that roan we saw in Leadville."

The lodge itself showed no sign of life except smoke from a stone chimney. "How do we gun 'em out?" Murray puzzled. "If we rush 'em they'll take it out on the girls."

"I've got an idea," Collier said. "Let's get upcreek from them."

Trees screened them as they continued to detour the lodge and move uphill. Presently they struck the creek at a spot where, due to the steepness of its course, it was higher than the lodge roof.

"Look for an intake pipe," John Collier suggested. "A man who spends that much money on a house isn't going to carry water in buckets. He'd pipe it in by gravity."

In a pool above the next waterfall they found an intake. A two-inch pipe led from the pool and disappeared underground in the direction of the lodge. Around the end of the pipe was a wire mesh calculated to keep out gravel and silt.

Collier took a pry pole and waded into the pool. When the others saw his purpose they found poles and went in to help him. In twenty minutes they'd pried away the screen and raised the pipe's end to a level where water could no longer flow into it.

"Okay, Gerry. Now let's hide and wait."

Each deputy picked a fir tree and stood behind it. When inmates of the lodge found their water shut off they'd surely send someone here to find out why. "That way we get a blue chip of our own," Collier said. "Maybe three of 'em."

# Twenty-three

A cloud filmed the sky, hiding the sun. An hour went by and Collier, wet to the knees, stood shivering back of his tree. From here he couldn't see the lodge but Gerry Harlan, from another vantage point, could see part of it.

"They're a long time coming," Monte fretted impatiently.

"It won't do us much good," Gerry said, "unless they all three come at once."

Collier had to admit it. Even if two of the men came to the intake and were knocked down without firing a shot, there'd still be one gunman in the house; a killer outlaw with the power of life or death over two prisoners. Any threat or attempt at rescue would make him use that power. The last line of a warning message came brutally back to Collier: "If you make trouble for us you'll never see them again."

He stamped the ground to get the chill out of his legs.

"Must be close to noon," Murray guessed. "When the woman starts to cook grub for 'em she'll need water."

And when she turned on a faucet no water would come; or only what was stored in the pipe, which would come with diminishing pressure.

Another tedious wait and then a hushed warning from Harlan. "Someone's coming! He's got a shovel and he's wearing hip boots."

"Only one man?"

"Only one."

Collier swallowed his disappointment. "Don't shoot. And don't let him see us. Just bat him down."

He could see the oncomer himself now. The boots came to his thighs and above the waist he wore a tight-fitting turtleneck sweater. The sweater was black and so was his droopy-brimmed hat. The hat kept Collier from seeing more than the lower half of his face.

"He's not Buckshot Joe," Harlan whispered.

The shovel which the man carried over his shoulder suggested that there'd been intake trouble before. After a freshet from melting snow, sand or gravel might clog the screen and keep water from entering the pipe. The man with the boots and shovel could wade out and clear away any such obstruction.

As he came nearer Collier saw a little more of his face. It was a swarthy, foreign face and he knew he'd seen it before. But where?

The man had crossed the lodge clearing now and was into the creek-bank conifers. He passed within a pace of Murray's tree and got no farther. The rifle barrel which crashed on his head gave no chance for an outcry. The man fell stunned to the ground and Harlan said, "Nice work, Monte."

Collier stooped, turned the man face up, removed the black hat. "Look, Gerry! We saw him at the Clarendon one time. He brought in some drinks, remember?"

"He's Lippo," Gerry said after a close look. "Works for Flint Hammond."

The significance of it struck all three of them at once. Monte swore softly. "Up jumps the devil! Now we know who's backin' this play. The payoff man! But what the hell's Hammond got against *you,* Johnnie?"

Collier stared vacantly at Lippo. "I don't know, Monte. Probably the same thing he had against Bryson. Right now it doesn't matter. Nothing matters except getting the girls out of that house."

"Monk and Buckshot are still in there," Gerry brooded. "When Lippo doesn't go back, maybe they'll come to see why. And we can gun 'em down."

"Only one would come," Collier thought. "Or they might send the woman." It would leave at least one man in there to hold a gun on Angela and Lola.

"And he'd as lief shoot 'em as look at 'em," Murray said.

"Only one way to best them," Collier concluded. He kneeled by the stunned Lippo and pulled off the man's hip boots.

While his friends wondered what he was up to, he took off his own riding boots and put on the hip-high water boots. He drew them up around his thighs and a minute later was slipping Lippo's black turtleneck sweater over his head. "Lippo's about my build and height, Gerry."

He picked up the shovel and slanted it over his shoulder. "How do I look, Monte?"

"You're *loco,* Johnnie. You look about as much like Lippo as I look like Queen Victoria! They'd know you in a minute."

"Not with this hat on." Collier put on Lippo's hat and let the limber brim of it sag over his forehead and eyes. He looked up at a gray sky. "The light's not very good, either. Seeing me from a window they'll think I'm Lippo coming back. I can be inside face to face with 'em before they know better."

Gerry Harlan didn't think so. "You'd never get away with it, Johnnie. They'd drill you before you got halfway to the house."

"They'd know you by your gun," Monte put in. Lippo had come to the intake armed only with a shovel.

Collier took off his gunbelt and dropped it. Then he took the gun from its holster and wedged it under the sweater at his back. "I won't let them see it," he promised, "till I'm inside. It's past noon. Chances are they're in the kitchen eating."

"You'll get your fool head shot off," Murray insisted.

"Stay here, Johnnie," Harlan begged, "and let *me* go."

"No, Gerry. You're half a head taller than Lippo. And Monte's too chunky at the middle. You fellas can cover me, if you want, while I take the walk. But don't shoot unless they shoot first. Which door did Lippo come out of?"

"The back door."

"Then that's the way I'll go in. Wish me luck, pardners."

With the hatbrim pulled low and the shovel over his shoulder, John Collier walked straight toward the house.

A dozen steps took him out of the trees and into the lodge clearing. There were windows on this side, both upstairs and down.

From an upper window Angela or Lola might see him. Their jailers could spot him from a lower window if they happened to look out. Two outlaws named Buckshot and Monk—gangmen killers in the pay of Flint Hammond.

Hammond who'd offered them a bonus for the life of John Collier! Snipers in that crew had shot at him many times from the dark, in Leadville. Now he advanced steadily toward them, his hip boots swishing, an easy target from any window.

At the tree line behind him Monte and Gerry were aiming rifles at those windows. But their triggers were leashed. Any long-distance shooting would imperil Angela and Lola.

John Collier pulled the hatbrim lower, shifted the shovel to his other shoulder and walked with his head slightly bowed. Were they looking at him? He angled toward the lodge's back door, now thirty steps from it, now twenty, now ten. There was a rear porch with firewood stacked on it. A door there probably gave to a kitchen.

As he gained the porch he made no effort to be quiet. Instead he stamped his feet and let the shovel fall with a clang. A man's voice in the kitchen said: "I hear Lippo coming back. See if you can draw some water, Marta."

Then a woman's voice: "Before you come in, Lippo, take off those wet boots."

Collier reached behind him and took a forty-five gun from under his sweater. His right hand held it while his left opened the door. Even then they didn't at once see him. An enormous woman stood at a sink turning on a water faucet. Two men were eating at a table, one shaggy and robust, the other smooth and lean.

The shaggy man looked up first. For a breath he was petrified by the shock of seeing an aimed gun in a hand which wasn't Lippo's. His yell, "Look out, Monk!" came a second too late as he jumped to his feet and drew.

Collier tripped his own trigger twice, then swung his aim on Monk.

Monk drew without getting up. But he was sitting too close to the table and the edge of it caught the tip of his gun barrel as it came level. Collier fired again, aiming breast high, then again swung his aim toward Buckshot Joe Wofford.

He didn't need to fire. As Wofford sagged to the floor the woman at the sink screamed. She broke into an hysteria of mixed English and Italian. "Where is Lippo?" she pleaded.

A pounding of running feet announced the approach of Harlan and Murray. They catapulted into the kitchen with cocked rifles.

Collier motioned toward the table. "I think I got them both, Gerry." He turned to the woman. "Let me have your keys, Marta."

House keys hung from a ring at her belt. When she made no move to hand them over, Collier snatched them and rushed forward into a hallway, looking for stairs.

He raced up them, shouting: "Angela! Lola! Where are you?"

Angela's voice answered from beyond an upper door. "In here, Johnnie. Are you all right?"

He unlocked the door and there she was, not haggard and bruised as he'd feared. Backed against a far wall stood Lola, her face tear-streaked and bloodless. But whatever terrors had held Angela were gone now. Whatever poise she'd lost was instantly restored as a man who loved her but whose name she didn't know, or need to know just now, came toward her with open arms.

The lodge buckboard creaked slowly down a trail to the fork, and there met the Cottonwood Pass wagon road. It was after sundown and a cool breath of mountain twilight breathed on them from the aspens. Gerry Harlan drove with Lola on the front seat by him. Angela shared the back seat with John Collier. Two saddled horses followed, their lead ropes tied to the endgate. Monte Murray came last on horseback leading two other mounts, each with a prisoner in its saddle.

The woman prisoner alternately moaned and pleaded, tears on her broad fleshy face. "They will put us in jail, Lippo." Lippo himself rode in sullen silence, wristbound. His only words had been: "Be quiet, Marta. We tell nothing."

"I doubt if she knows anything to tell, Johnnie," Angela said. "I'm sure she was never in Leadville. They never confided in her. She's strong as an ox and simple as a child. The names Janford and Culp mean nothing to her."

"Did she ever mention Flint Hammond?"

"No. I feel sure she never saw Hammond. All she seemed to know was that she and her husband would be shipped back to Italy and put in jail unless she did exactly what Lippo told her to do. We could hear men talking below stairs but she never let them see us, or us them. Always she was polite and protective. And always she promised that on a certain date we would be set free unharmed."

"And you believed her?"

"Not at first. But finally we decided she's too stupid to lie convincingly. After that we weren't very much afraid any more."

"Your father is. He's just about given up all hope."

"I'll send him a telegram," Angela said, "when we get to Buena Vista."

The prospect worried Collier. "Pull up a minute, Gerry, and let's talk this over."

When the buckboard stopped he asked, "You wouldn't want Hammond to get away, would you?"

"Of course not," Angela said quickly.

Harlan echoed her. "Sure we don't. He's earned a high hanging, that guy has."

"You'll be giving him a four-hour start," Collier warned them, "if you report by telegraph from Buena Vista. The Leadville operator'll know it; the messenger boy who delivers the wire'll know it; everybody in the telegraph office and the sheriff's office will know. Your father will shout his joy to the world, Angela. News like this is too big to keep buttoned up. Hammond'll hear it; by the time I get to Leadville he'll be long gone."

"But we mustn't let him!" Lola exclaimed.

"I should say not!" Gerry agreed vigorously.

Murray rode up and was no less insistent. The man who'd backed the killings of Bryson and Cal Barstow and put a bounty on John Collier's head, and whose personal servant had imprisoned two girls, must not at any cost be permitted to escape.

"The sure way to stop him," Collier said, "is for me to beat the news to Leadville. If I take off from here with the two fastest horses, I can make it by midnight."

"Why *you?*" Gerry objected. "Let *me* make the ride."

The same offer came from Monte Murray but Collier was stubborn about it. "It's my party," he said. "None of this devilment would've happened if I hadn't come to Leadville. I still don't know why; or who the heck I am; or why Hammond wants me dead. But I started it all and I've got a right to finish it. Pick out the best two horses for me, Monte. If I cut north to the stage road from here I won't need to go through Buena Vista."

All the arguments they could bring to bear didn't shake him. "Angela and I," Lola Loomis said finally, "could stay at the Buena Vista hotel all night and catch the morning stage to Leadville."

"Or I can drive you there," Harlan said. "Monte, you'll need to steer Potter out to the lodge to clean up things." The bodies of Monk and Buckshot had been left locked in the lodge.

"And you, Gerry," Collier said urgently, "will have to sit on the Buena Vista operator for the next five hours. Make sure he doesn't send out anything even if you have to cut the wires."

He got out of the buckboard and stepped into the saddle of a horse. Murray handed him the lead rope of a remount. "I'll tell your father, Angela," he promised, "soon as we get Hammond locked up."

John Collier leaned from the saddle to kiss her good-bye. "Take good care of 'em, Gerry." Then he dug in with his spurs and was off on a fast forced ride to Leadville.

# Twenty-four

At the same twilight hour Flint Hammond took his regular table in the Clarendon dining room. From a corner of his eye he saw that Mel Janford was already there. The lawyer's dinner wine hadn't yet been served. Hammond had no doubt but that it would be the usual claret. Everything had gone quietly today and Janford, although eating a bit hurriedly and a little earlier than usual, didn't seem disturbed about anything.

Hammond ordered a steak and waiting for it he acknowledged nods and greetings from nearby tables. Mr. Corbett of the Utah smelter stopped by to congratulate him on a record assay of the *Morning Star* ore. The manager of the new Tabor Opera House handed him a pair of tickets for the grand opening due soon, with the compliments of Mr. Tabor himself.

The steak came and Hammond was using his knife on it when again he looked obliquely across the room toward Janford.

A waitress was serving wine to Janford. *It wasn't red, but white!* Sherry tonight instead of claret!

With conspicuous deliberation the lawyer raised his wine glass, drank from it, then over the top of it looked meaningly at Flint Hammond. It was a clear and certain signal! They must meet, tonight, at the *Evening Star* shanty.

So something was up, after all! That nosy lawyer had smelled trouble somewhere. Trouble serious enough to impel a long cold night ride to Breece Hill, and a conference there with Flint Hammond.

In a minute Mel Janford got up and walked out, leaving half his wine in the glass. It served to emphasize the signal.

Hammond didn't immediately follow. His own departure must not seem connected with Janford's. Let Janford get to the meeting place first and wait for him.

It was nearly dark when Hammond reached his livery stable and had them saddle up. Riding out of town he assumed he was about twenty minutes behind Janford.

What could the man want? Did it have anything to do with those three deputies from rooms 276 and 278? Hammond hadn't seen them all day. But they could hardly have uncovered anything. This evening's paper had mentioned no break in the search for Gus Culp. There could be nothing new in the abduction mystery for the face of County Clerk Rand, at dinner tonight, had mirrored only the usual hopeless dejection.

Hammond spurred to a lope, by-passing Fryer Hill and pushing on to Breece. He kept clear of the productive areas there and angled to a deserted rincon which showed only a single light. It would be a lantern in the *Evening Star* shanty and it proved that Janford was already there, waiting.

In the shed he found Janford's horse and tied his own beside it. Clouds screened the stars, making the night too dark to see even the silhouette of a long-abandoned winch at the mine shaft. More than seven months had gone by since an ore bucket had been hoisted from that shaft. According to the county records, half of this almost worthless property still belonged to the estate of Job Norcross.

Except for a gleam of a lantern there, Hammond would have needed to grope his way to the shanty. Entering, he saw Janford sitting on a stool and puffing a cigaret.

"What's up, Janford?"

"I need some keys," the lawyer said. The smile on his lips gave them a cynical twist.

"What keys?"

"The ones on your keyring. Let's have them." The lawyer held out his hand, palm up; and now, in the dim lantern light, his smile seemed far more sinister than cynical.

A chill bit Hammond as he backed toward the door. What stopped him was a pressure against the middle of his back. It had the feel of a small metal circle and could only be the bore of a gun.

This wasn't a meeting; it was a trap! In a nausea

of panic Flint Hammond looked over his shoulder and saw the face of Gus Culp. Not only a trap, but a death trap! Culp's hand pressed harder with the gun.

Then Hammond was aware of another hand, Janford's, dipping into his pocket. There was a jingle as the hand came out.

The lawyer held up a ring of keys. "We'll only need three of them, Gus: the one to his suite at the Clarendon; the one to his office there; and the one to his office safe."

With the breath of death on him Flint Hammond began a frantic pleading. "Wait, Janford! I'll up your per cent. I'll give you half."

"You'll give us *all*," the lawyer broke in curtly. "And it's all there, bonds and cash. You've been stuffing it in there for a month. Finish him off, Gus; then drop him in the shaft."

Culp squeezed his trigger once, and once was enough.

Darkness caught Collier as he crossed Three Elk Creek and at Four Elk Creek he struck the stage road. No reason he couldn't make Leadville by midnight. At that hour Hammond, if unwarned, should be in bed and asleep. Yanking him out of it and hustling him to a cell would be a grim and pressing pleasure.

Certainly it was a thing which couldn't wait. The night had eyes and ears and some Culper still at large might at this very minute be riding hard to warn Hammond.

At Harvard Creek Collier stopped to shift his saddle. But he was no sooner on the remount when he realized it was limping slightly. He got down, looked under all four hooves for a wedged stone and found none.

Impatiently he shifted the saddle again. Leading a lame horse would only slow him so he turned it loose by the trail.

After that he had to walk his mount more than half the time. At Granite he asked for a fresh horse but the station corral had nothing but harness stock. While Collier rested and grained the animal he had, the stage for Canon City stopped to make a relay change. It was the same coach on which Angela and Lola had set forth so gaily for Denver.

A clicking of the station telegraph key spurred Collier and made him ride on fast. Night operators led a lonely life and liked to gossip with each other. In spite of all Gerry Harlan's vigilance the operator at Buena Vista might talk to this one, or to Leadville.

At the mouth of Twin Lakes Creek the horse began blowing and had to be walked for a few miles. The road seemed endless to Collier, dark and soundless except for the rushing river at his right. He crossed it on a wooden bridge and pushed to a trot again. Mile after weary mile. It was midnight when the glow of the Malta smelter came in sight.

Collier passed the smelter without stopping, turning up California Gulch. Along it he passed three other smelters, all with night crews and running full blast.

As he struck the foot of Chestnut Street Collier's watch said one o'clock. Tucker would be home and in bed. The sheriff's office would have only a night desk man on duty and Collier was in no mood to trust underlings. There'd been leaks from that office. He could handle Hammond himself and Collier was determined to do just that. Hammond the paymaster of murderers! A millionaire thief, Ada Culp called him. Hammond the high-flying hypocrite! *He even offered to pay my room and board!*

Turning up Harrison Collier once more forced his nearly spent mount to a lope. The street was full and noisy. Men who knew him by sight hailed him from the sidewalks but he didn't answer. At the Clarendon he drew up and tied his horse.

As he went into the lobby sheer weariness made him stumble. In the last twenty-three hours he'd ridden eighty miles.

The sleepy night clerk on duty was the same one who'd seen him leave last night with Murray and Harlan.

For the first time since Tucker had given it to him, John Collier took a deputy's badge from his pocket and displayed it in the palm of his hand.

"I've got to make an arrest," he told the night clerk.

The clerk's mouth hung open. "Yeh? Who you gonna pinch, Mr. Collier?"

"The man has a room here. Give me a master key so I can walk in on him." Collier held out his hand. His voice, sternly imperative, matched the haggardness of his face and the clerk sensed it was a crisis in the Culp manhunt. He'd been instructed by the management to show every courtesy to a trio of county deputies assigned to rooms 276 and 278.

"Yes sir." The clerk took a master key from a drawer and passed it across the desk.

With it John Collier went bounding up the stairs. At the top he turned down the south wing corridor toward the suite of Flint Hammond. A deep carpet muffled his steps. He stopped at a door with a silver horseshoe over it. A shoe made from *Morning Star* silver! *Your luck's running out, Hammond.*

Collier put his key in the lock, turned it cautiously, hoping to surprise Hammond in his sleep. He pushed the door open and entered a dark sitting room where rugs again muffled his step.

But a door beyond showed a crack of light at the bottom. It was the door to Hammond's home office. Since the office was lighted, the man was probably working late in there.

John Collier pinned Tucker's badge on his jacket and drew his gun. After advancing softly to the office door he put his hand on the knob. Then he heard a low voice beyond it; a voice which wasn't Hammond's.

So Hammond had a visitor! Could it be Janford?

Pausing for a moment, Collier strained his ears to catch words. Yes, the voice was Janford's but the words seemed unimportant. *"It's no good to us; throw it away."*

Throw what away? Collier didn't wait to hear more. He opened the door and stepped quietly into the office, gun level.

Two men were there. One, Janford, was kneeling in front of an open safe. He was raking bonds and currency from the safe and stuffing them into a grain sack which a second man was holding open. Already the sack was nearly full.

"Only a little more of it, Gus; then we can ride." The exulting words were Janford's.

The next were John Collier's. *"What happened to Hammond?"*

Janford spun about and saw an aimed gun. A reflex of his shock jarred a cry from him. *"Look out, Gus. It's Warren!"*

Gus Culp dropped the sack and slapped at the grip of his gun. It was half out when Collier fired twice, dropping him.

If Janford had a gun he didn't try to use it. Still on his knees at the safe and with his face ash-white, the lawyer reached out his arms pleadingly. "Don't shoot, Warren! For God's sake don't shoot!"

"Thanks," Wesley Warren said, "for telling me my name."

On the floor lay a paper with a red wax seal and the look of a legal document. "Is this what you told Gus to throw away?"

Stooping, Wesley Warren picked up the paper. A notarized signature at the bottom of it was "Job Norcross."

"Thanks again, Janford. Makes me remember I had an Uncle Job. Things are clearing up a little."

Shouts and running footsteps sounded from the hall. The two shots had been heard by other guests and from the lobby.

Wesley Warren raised his voice to call them in. In a few minutes a dozen shocked witnesses were crowding into the office. One of them was a constable who'd been patrolling Harrison. Wesley Warren knew him by sight and name.

"Take over here, Conway. The dead man's Gus Culp. He was helping Janford strip the safe. Put everything back and lock it up."

When he'd made himself clear Wesley Warren brushed past them. He hurried down to the lobby and out to his horse. Bone-weary, he climbed into the saddle for his last forced ride of the night. It was a short one, only half a mile up Harrison to a house on Capitol Hill.

The man who lived there, aroused from a troubled sleep, answered his knock. His stare was unbending, his voice cold. "What are *you* doing here, Collier?"

"The name's Warren and I've got good news, Mr. Rand. We located Angela and Lola. They're both okay and 'll be home on the morning stage."

# Twenty-five

The Clarendon ballroom, because it had an organ and was the only room in town large enough and handsome enough for the purpose, was selected by Milton Rand for a high-noon ceremony early in October. Chairs were provided for two hundred guests, and all were occupied well before the hour.

An overflow peered in from the lobby and among these were Sheriff Tucker, City Marshal Duggan, and Deputies Murray and Trevor. They'd lingered too long at the bar, drinking the bride's health, and had emerged too late to find seats.

Looking in they saw the elite of Leadville waiting in solemn quiet for the first notes of the organ. Out here in the lobby there was a hum of talk among the uninvited, while beyond a row of potted palms a trio of fiddlers from the Tabor Opera House, soon to open across the street,

266

made gentle music. Proprietor William Bush was sparing no effort to make it a gala occasion.

"What's that cowboy gonna do with all his money?" Duggan wondered. "They claim he'll assay out at more'n a million."

Monte Murray, a close confidant of Wesley Warren, had the answer. "He's gonna buy out the F Bar, hoof, horn and acre."

"Where's that?" Trevor inquired.

"It's where he punched cows before he came here," Monte told them. "A forty-thousand-acre layout in Cheyenne County, Nebraska, near the Wyoming line. Wes says his old boss wants to sell out and retire. Six thousand head of stock on it."

Trevor gave a low whistle. "It'd take a mint of money to buy an outfit like that."

"Which is what Wes'll have, once they get this *Morning Star* mess cleaned up in his favor. He says he'd heap rather run cows on top the ground than dig for silver under it. Once a cowboy, always a cowboy, they say."

"Who'll do the cleanin' up for him? I mean the legal mess."

"That Poplar Street lawyer named Gentry," Monte said. "Wes'll get a lot of help from Milt Rand too. Milt's already written to a Kaycee notary and got proof that the *Morning Star* title was jimmied. Not only that, when you look close at the 'Mor' in the deed you can see it was put there after someone rubbed out 'Eve.' It's open and shut, Gentry and Rand say. Half of everything that ever came out of the mine'll be awarded to Wes—plus any damages he wants to claim from Hammond's estate."

Barry Holden of the *Chronicle* appeared and joined them, out of breath. "Big news, Sheriff. They just found Hammond's body."

"Where?" Tucker asked.

"At the bottom of the *Evening Star* shaft. A bullet hole through him. Not only that, but a wire just came in from Salt Lake City. They nabbed two more Culpers on their way to Nevada."

"That," Tucker said, "just about washes 'em up. I've got Janford and Lippo in jail; and Wes wants to go easy on Marta."

Duggan asked, "What about Culp's wife, Ada?"

"As a special favor to Angela Rand we'll go easy on her too. Fact is we haven't even bothered to pick her up."

"She had Janford and Hammond pegged just right," Trevor said. "Called 'em a swindling blackmailer and a millionaire thief."

"Pipe down!" Barry cautioned. "The show's starting."

They looked into the ballroom and saw Tom Uzzell enter at the rear, accompanied by Wesley Warren and his tall friend, Gerry Harlan. Uzzell, who often preached in barrooms and on street corners, was Leadville's most active and respected clergyman.

Trevor chuckled as he nudged Murray. "Look at Gerry! He's rigged out fit to kill! A wonder that high wing collar don't choke him."

"Shh!" Monte whispered as an organist began the wedding march.

A door at the top end of the ballroom opened and Angela appeared on the arm of her father. A stately brunette, Lola Loomis, walked behind them as maid of honor. Reaching a center aisle the three moved in slow cadence down it toward the minister.

Angela, radiant in her long gown and veil, left her father to take Wes Warren's hand. They stood before the minister with Gerry and Lola on either side.

Monte Murray looked from Gerry to Lola and then buzzed a whisper to the ear of Barry Holden. "It'll be *their* turn next, from what I hear."

Barry was too good a reporter to miss a lead like that. He whipped out a notebook. "If you've got any inside dope, Monte, let's have it."

"All I know, Barry, is that Wes offered Gerry a job as foreman of the F Bar; and Gerry says he'll take it if he can talk Lola into living on a ranch."

The minister began his ritual and the five friends at the lobby doorway listened attentively till itwas over. As the groom kissed the bride, Monte whispered something to Barry Holden which brought a grin to the reporter's face. The two backed away and disappeared in the lobby crowd.

"Wonder what those two monkeys are up to," Tucker muttered to Duggan.

An hour later he and all of Leadville found out. They stood in a dense press on the walk in front of the Clarendon. Drawn up there was a team of matched grays harnessed to the city's shiniest buckboard. The vehicle's rear seat had been removed to make room for the bride's baggage.

Tucker, Duggan and Trevor were there, as well as Milton Rand and all the other county officers. A brass band was ready to serenade the departing couple.

Everyone was there, it seemed to Tucker, except Monte Murray and Barry Holden.

Then Angela came out in the smart traveling suit and hat to which she'd changed, her cheeks flushed happily as she held to Wes Warren's arm. With his free hand Warren swept a path across the walk to the buckboard. Milton Rand stood there to kiss his daughter good-bye. He shook hands with Wesley Warren.

"Come to see us at the F bar," Wes invited heartily. He handed Angela to the buckboard seat, then got in himself and gathered up the reins.

"It'll be a long ride for them," Duggan remarked to Tucker, "up over Mosquito Pass and down to End-of-Track."

"They won't mind it, Duggan. After that they can ride the cushions all the way to Nebraska."

Wesley Warren snapped the reins and the rig rolled off down Harrison. "It's some different from the last time," Tucker said. "Remember? He was lyin' in a wagon bed with a bashed head, behind run-away mules. . . . What's that hangin' on behind, Duggan?"

Barry and Monte joined them, grinning guiltily. "We didn't have any cowbells or old shoes," Monte said.

"Hope it brings them better luck than it did Hammond," Barry chuckled.

Swinging from the buckboard's endgate was the silver horseshoe which had hung over Flint Hammond's door.

**Center Point Large Print**
600 Brooks Road / PO Box 1
Thorndike, ME 04986-0001 USA

**(207) 568-3717**

**US & Canada:**
**1 800 929-9108**
www.centerpointlargeprint.com